D1547110

The Realest Killaz 2

Tranay Adams

**Lock Down Publications and Ca$h
Presents**
The Realest Killaz 2
A Novel by *Tranay Adams*

Lock Down Publications
P.O. Box 944
Stockbridge, Ga 30281

Copyright 2020 by Tranay Adams
The Realest Killaz 2

First Edition October 2020
Printed in the United States of America

Lock Down Publications
Like our page on Facebook: Lock Down Publications @
www.facebook.com/lockdownpublications.ldp
Cover design and layout by: **Dynasty Cover Me**
Book interior design by: **Shawn Walker**
Edited by: **Nuel Uyi**

Stay Connected with Us!

Text **LOCKDOWN** to 22828 to stay up-to-date with new releases, sneak peaks, contests and more...

Thank you!

Submission Guideline.

Submit the first three chapters of your completed manuscript to ldpsubmissions@gmail.com, subject line: Your book's title. The manuscript must be in a .doc file and sent as an attachment. Document should be in Times New Roman, double spaced and in size 12 font. Also, provide your synopsis and full contact information. If sending multiple submissions, they must each be in a separate email.

Have a story but no way to send it electronically? You can still submit to LDP/Ca$h Presents. Send in the first three chapters, written or typed, of your completed manuscript to:

LDP: Submissions Dept
P.O. Box 944
Stockbridge, Ga 30281

DO NOT send original manuscript. Must be a duplicate.

Provide your synopsis and a cover letter containing your full contact information.

Thanks for considering LDP and Ca$h Presents.

Tranay Adams

Chapter 1

Joaquin strolled out the jail facility, dressed in the same shit he was in when he was arrested. He wore a smile across his lips, as he looked up at the beaming sun, listening to the afternoon traffic and the birds chirping. He took a deep breath and exhaled. A moment later, he saw a black on black Navigator limousine on twenty-eight-inch chrome rims and tires. The car drove close up. The driver's door opened, and the chauffeur stepped out. He made his way around the enormous SUV and stepped upon the curb, where Joaquin could see him in his entirety. The chauffeur, who also acted as a bodyguard, was a six-foot-two Mexican cat, wearing black sunglasses. He had a monstrous tattooed head and a massive body covered in muscles. The South American man was dressed in a black blazer, black jeans and snakeskin cowboy boots, with silver skulls on the tips of them.

"Are you Mr. Torres?" the bodyguard asked with a smile, revealing a mouth full of silver teeth, which gleamed from the rays of the sun.

"Yeah, but chu can call me Joaquin," Joaquin replied.

"I'm Hugo, Joaquin." Hugo extended his hand, which Joaquin shook. Joaquin noticed he was wearing a silver skull ring, which matched the skulls on his boots. "My boss, Mr. Alvaro, sent me to pick you up. He gave me orders to take you wherever you'd like to go. He also told me to give you this—" he pulled a fat ass envelope out of his blazer and presented it to Joaquin. When Joaquin opened it, he saw it was loaded with blue face one hundred dollar bills. "He wants you to get reacquainted with the outside world for the day. Go shopping, buy yourself some things, and enjoy some festivities. Afterwards, he'd like for you to come out and see em, whenever you're ready—no rush."

"Okay, Hugo," Joaquin began, sliding the envelope inside his blazer. "The first thing I needa get my hands on is a gun. A clean one—preferably with a silencer."

"Oh, I can get that for you. No problem."

"Good."

"Where would you like to go first?"

"I'm hungry as a hostage. I'd like some really good Mexican food." Joaquin rubbed his stomach. "I'm talking *real* Mexican food. Not that Americanized shit that Del Taco and Taco Bell serves either. That shit is god-fucking-awful!"

"I know just the place," Hugo said. "Shall we leave?" He motioned to the Navigator with his massive hand.

"Yeah, let's get outta here. If I stay out here any longer, these gringos may wanna lock me back up." Joaquin glanced back at the facility he'd just exited, as he unbuttoned his blazer and stepped off the curb. Hugo held open the back door for Joaquin. Joaquin was about to get in, until two beautiful Afro-Brazilian women stuck their heads out of the door. They were dressed in skimpy bikinis that showed off their voluptuous bodies. The women smiled sexily at Joaquin and flicked their tongues against each other's. They then sucked each other's tongues and kissed sensually.

Joaquin's forehead wrinkled. He looked from the enticing women to Hugo, wondering what the big idea was. "What's this?" he asked of the women that were obviously meant for him.

"This," Hugo smiled and motioned to the Brazilian beauties, "is your festivities." He produced a row of six gold-foil-wrapped lubricated condoms, and passed them to Joaquin. Joaquin smiled, took the condoms, and slid into the back seat of the stretch Navigator. Once he slammed the door behind him, Hugo walked around to the driver's side and hopped in. He cranked up the enormous SUV and pulled into traffic, driving off.

***

That night

God, Billie and the girls sat on the couch, under a blanket, eating popcorn and laughing at *Frozen 2*. The doorbell chimed and stole God and Billie's attention. They looked at the door, then back at each other.

"Pizza," God and Billie said in unison.

"Mommy, we're all outta popcorn," Annabelle told her mother and flashed the big empty bowl, with popcorn residue in it.

Billie took the bowl and looked to God. "I'll get the popcorn while you get the pizza, deal?" She extended her fist toward him.

"Deal." God dapped her up. They then kissed, threw the blankets off them and went separate ways. Billie went to the kitchen and God went to the front door.

The doorbell chimed once again.

"I'm coming, I'm coming! God said, as he approached the door, pulling a knot of one hundred dollar bills from out of his pocket.

"Bae!" Billie called out to God from inside of the kitchen.

"What's up?" God asked, preparing to move the chain from the front door.

"Don't forget the Pepsi."

"Okay," he responded, removing the chain from the door and unlocking the lock. He twisted the knob and pulled open the door. His eyes doubled in size, his mouth hanging open, when he saw Joaquin standing on the other side.

Joaquin smiled at him wickedly while holding his right hand behind his back. Suddenly, his eyebrows arched and his nose scrunched up, a vein on his temple bulged. He brought his right hand up and pointed a SIG Sauer P226 with a silencer in God's face.

"I told you to stay the fuck away from my family, or I'd kill you, didn't I?"

"Mommy, is that daddy?" Annabelle asked her mother. She couldn't see Joaquin clearly, and the gun he was pointing wasn't visible to her.

"Joaquin?" Billie inquired. She sounded like it was hard for her to believe that her daughter's father was at her door.

"Lucky motherfucker," Joaquin said while mad-dogging God. A smile spread across his face, and he held his SIG Sauer P226 behind his back.

"It is my daddy! Annabelle said jovially. "Daddyyyyyy!"

Annabelle hopped off the couch and took off, running toward Joaquin. He scooped her up in one arm and she hugged him around his neck, kissing him all over his face sweetly. Joaquin smiled, enjoying the warm affection he received from his daughter.

"Joaquin, when did you get out?" Billie asked, as she approached the door. She was about to pop the popcorn when she heard Joaquin was at the door. Upon hearing that, she hurried out of the kitchen and stood beside God, with Charity holding her arm around her neck.

"Earlier today," Joaquin replied, kissing Annabelle up and down her cheek, causing her to laugh and giggle.

"You're so silly, daddy." Annabelle smiled happily, laying the side of her head against his and hugging his neck.

"Well, why didn't you call me?" Billie said. "I woulda picked you up."

"It's all good, baby mama, a friend of mine sent his chauffeur to give me a lift."

"Oh, okay."

Joaquin discretely tucked his gun into the small of his back, without anyone noticing him. "Now, are you going to leave me out here in the cold, or are you gonna invite me in?"

"My bad,—um, excuse my manners—Please come in," Billie said and nudged God. He opened the door wider so Joaquin could come inside.

Joaquin crossed the threshold, giving God an evil glare, looking him up and down like he wasn't shit. God did the same. Billie and Charity noticed the hostility and tension between them, but Billie didn't comment on it.

"Lemme introduce you to everyone," Billie said. "You already know the love of my life and my fiancé, Kyree."

"Yeah, I know 'em. What's up, nigga?" Joaquin said. He switched arms with Annabelle and extended his hand toward God.

God mad-dogged Joaquin and clenched his teeth tightly, showcasing the bones in his jaws. His stare was so intense he could have burned a hole through Joaquin for the stunt he'd pulled.

The audacity of this punk mothafucka to come up in my crib and shove a fucking gun in my face. He must don't think fat meat greasy, but he's gonna find out! Oh, yeah, he's definitely gone find out! God thought, as he reluctantly shook Joaquin's hand.

Joaquin and Billie had broken up while he was fighting an attempted murder case in jail. One night, while they were out at a very popular club, Billie had caught Joaquin fucking some skeezer in the women's rest room. Billie lost it and whipped homegirl's ass before returning to the dance floor.

The girl's girlfriends came to her aid inside the rest room and called the police. When Joaquin came out of the club, looking for Billie so they could split before Los Angeles' Finest showed up, he found her flirting with a handsome young man by the name of Antoine. Enraged, Joaquin grabbed his gun out of his car and started licking shots at him. He winded up wounding old boy, but he hadn't been successful in killing him.

The Boys in Blue came after Joaquin and he fled, ditching his gun inside a trash bin in an alley. He made his return to the public, acting like everything was fine and dandy. Unfortunately for him, the cops snatched him up and threw his black ass in jail. Joaquin was looking at some time, but he came up with a plan that could get his ass out of the fire. He had Joel Murtaugh—a corrections officer he'd formed a bond with while incarcerated—pay off Antoine so he wouldn't come to court and testify against him. It all worked out in Joaquin's favor; so here he was now—a free man.

Before Joaquin had gotten his walking papers, God had come up to see him while he was locked up. He wanted him to know that he and Billie would be getting married. Jealous and fearful of losing his family, Joaquin threatened God to stay away from his family, or he'd kill him. Being a man of his word, and even more a gangsta of his standing, Joaquin showed up at God's crib, strapped, looking to make good on his threat.

"And this beautiful lil' girl is Charity, my other daughter." Billie kneeled down to Charity, smiling and hugging her to her side. "Say hi to Annabelle's father, Charity."

Joaquin smiled down at Charity and extended his hand toward her. "Pleasure to meet chu, princess."

Charity was visibly afraid of Joaquin, and reasonably so. She'd seen him pointing a gun in her father's face. She'd seen enough to boil it down to Joaquin being a bad man. With the visual of Joaquin drawing down on her old man fresh in her mind, Charity hid behind God to avoid him.

Annabelle's brows furrowed, wondering why her soon-to-be stepsister was avoiding her father's greeting. "Charity, what's the matter? Why aren't you saying hi to my daddy?"

"It's okay, baby girl, lil' mama probably has been taught not to speak to strangers." Joaquin smirked.

"But you're notta stranger, you're my daddy," Annabelle told him.

"It's cool, baby, I'll eventually grow on her," Joaquin said, assuring Annabelle, kissing her on her cheek.

"I'll be back, I gotta take a leak," God said, keeping his eyes on Joaquin, as he kneeled down to Charity and kissed her on the side of her head.

Yeah, right, hijo de puta, you're not fooling nobody. You're going to get chu a strap, Joaquin thought, as he watched God disappear inside the hallway. He made a right, where he knew the bathroom was located, so he was sure he was going to get his gun.

"Daddy, would you like some ice cream?" Annabelle asked him.

"Have you been practicing your Spanish?" Joaquin fired back with a question of his own.

"Unh huh." Annabelle nodded.

"Well, ask me in Spanish then?" Joaquin told her.

Annabelle massaged her chin and looked up at the ceiling, thinking. Once she figured out how to ask her daddy what she had in mind in Spanish, she went on to ask him, "Quieres un helado, papi? (*Would you like some ice cream, daddy?*)"

Billie smiled, seeing Annabelle interact with her father in Spanish. He had been working on teaching her how to speak Spanish before he'd gotten locked up.

"Sí, me gustaría un poco de helado. Que tipo tienes? (*Yes, I'd like some ice cream. What kind do you have?*)"

"Tenemos mi favorito, papi, chispas de chocolate (*We have my favorite, daddy, chocolate chip*)."

"Nos pondré unas cucharadas en un tazón (*I'll put us a few scoops in a bowl*)," Billie told them. "Would you like some, Charity?"

"Yes." Charity spoke timidly.

"Okay, coming right up," Billie said, retreating inside the kitchen, with Charity on her heels.

Billie fixed everyone a bowl of chocolate chip ice cream—except God, who returned and sat at the kitchen table with them. Billie, Joaquin and Annabelle engaged in small talk, while God and Charity spent most of the time quiet. It wasn't long before Charity dozed off. God excused himself from the table and carried her into her bedroom. While he was gone, Billie continued conversing with Joaquin and Annabelle. Billie noticed how Joaquin and God had been glaring at each other while they were at the table, but she decided to bring it up at a later time. She could literally feel the tension in the air between them. In fact, the tension was so thick she could cut it with a knife.

"Lemme go get this phone," Billie said, hearing the telephone ringing inside her bedroom. She ate another spoonful of ice cream before getting up from the table.

Once Billie had disappeared from the kitchen, Joaquin texted Hugo to tell him he'd be out in another hour or so.

Hugo: *It's all good. No rush. Take your time.*

Joaquin was reading the message when he caught Annabelle looking over his shoulder at it. She smiled, realizing her father had caught her snooping. He smiled back at her and rubbed his nose against hers, kissing her on the forehead. Right then, there was a knock at the front door.

"Pizzaaaa!" Annabelle said excitedly, throwing her fists up in the air. She hopped off her father's lap and followed him to the front door.

"Who is it?" Joaquin called out.

"Pizza delivery!" the voice came from the other side.

"See, daddy, I told you it was the pizza." Annabelle smiled happily. She had smudges of chocolate chip ice cream around her mouth and on her cheek. Noticing this, Joaquin licked his thumb and got as much off of her as he could.

Joaquin pulled out the envelope of blue faces Hugo had blessed him with, and pulled out a one hundred dollar bill. Next, he unchained and unlocked the front door, pulling it open. He took the pizza from the delivery boy and passed him the one hundred dollar bill.

"That's all you," Joaquin told him, as he took the hot wings and the two liters of Pepsi from him. The delivery boy smiled graciously, thanking him, before pocketing the hefty tip and dipping off about his business.

Joaquin closed the door and told Annabelle to lock it. She did like her father had told her, and danced inside the kitchen. She watched as her father sat down a few plates on the kitchen table and started placing slices on them.

"Ummm mmmm, daddy, it smells delicious," Annabelle said, as she licked her lips and rubbed her hands together hungrily. She then tucked a paper towel inside her collar, and sat down beside her father. She took a bite of her slice and shut her eyes, smiling. Annabelle then danced in her seat, singing a song about finally having her pizza. "Dang, daddy, you tearing that pizza up," she said to Joaquin, seeing him devour the rest of his first slice in less than five minutes. He looked at her, smiling, and then wiped his mouth, swallowing down the food in his mouth.

"Mommy, Daddy, pizza is here!" Annabelle announced loudly so Billie and God could hear her. "You better come get it before daddy eats it all." She giggled and smiled.

Joaquin was just about to bite into his second slice of pizza when he heard his daughter refer to God as her father. His brows furrowed and he sat his pizza down, snatching the paper towel from out of his collar. He wiped his hands off with it and turned around to Annabelle. "Princess, what the fuck did you just refer to that punk-ass nigga in there that cho momma is seeing?" He leaned so close in her face that she could smell the tomato sauce, garlic and pepperoni on his breath. The sight of the hatred burning in her father's pupils had her wide eyed and spooked. Annabelle had never seen her father so angry and intimidating.

"I—I—I called—called him—d—daddy," a teary eyed Annabelle said and poked out her bottom lip. Afraid that her father would take off his belt and whip her ass with it, Annabelle slightly trembled.

"That's just what the fuck I thought!" Joaquin snarled and grabbed Annabelle tightly by her bottom jaw, causing her lips to pucker up. The pain she felt in her face made the tears fall from her eyes consistently. She held on to her father's strong hand for fear he'd squeeze her jaw bone so tightly that it would crumble like a stale cookie. "Lemme tell you something, Annabelle Torres, don't ever, ever in yo' life refer to that bitch-ass nigga as yo' daddy again! That nigga ain't cho goddamn daddy, I'm yo' mothafucking daddy! You come from me, is that understood?" Annabelle sniffled and cried harder. She took the time to quickly wipe her dripping eyes with the back of her hand, and then she nodded understandingly. "Nah, lemme hear you say it."

"You're my daddy, and I come from you," she said, her voice cracking with raw emotions.

"And don't chu forget it. Now, eat cho pizza!" Joaquin told her. He then watched as she slowly started to eat her pizza. It was obvious that after their altercation, she'd lost her appetite, but she was going to eat her slice anyway. She was afraid to tell him she wasn't hungry anymore because she didn't want to upset him again.

Billie entered the kitchen with a frown, looking back and forth between Joaquin and Annabelle. She could tell by the expressions on their faces that something was up. She just didn't know exactly what.

"What's the matter, baby girl? What happened?" Billie asked her daughter with concern. Annabelle was weeping loudly. Her nostrils were flaring, and her shoulders jumped up and down. She was highly upset.

"Ain't shit wrong with her lil' ass, her fucking feelings are just hurt—that's all!" Joaquin said, as he mad-dogged his daughter. Her calling God 'daddy' had really gotten under his skin and gotten him out of character. He was as hot as the oven on 350 degrees. First, that pussy-ass nigga, God, had taken his woman, and now he was trying to snatch his little princess from him. That was where he'd drawn the line! He couldn't let that no-good, bitch-stealing, crack-peddling son of a bitch take his heart from him. And Annabelle Torres was most definitely his heart! "That's some foul ass shit, Billie! You got my baby up in here calling another nigga 'daddy'? What kinda shit is that? How'd you like it if I had her calling some ho I was lying the pipe to 'momma'? You wouldn't be feeling that shit, would you? I know you, so I know you wouldn't. So, don't pull that shit with me!" He scowled at her, and his nostrils flared as he pointed his finger at her. His eyes were glassy and angry. He looked like he was about ready to get violent any second then.

"Hold up before you start going in on me!" an angry Billie shot back with mad attitude. She was moving her head from side to side like a stereotypical hood rat, and pointing her finger animatedly. "I did not have our daughter calling another man 'daddy'. If she was calling 'em that, then it was on her own accord. I didn't put her up to doing nothing! So miss me with all of that!"

"Yeah, whatever!" Joaquin spat with his face balled up heatedly, waving her off. He really wasn't trying to hear that bullshit she was trying to kick to him because he felt like he knew better.

Chapter 2

"Do we have a problem here?" God asked as he returned to the kitchen. His face was fixed with a concerned expression, and he looked like he was about to put hands on somebody.

Right then, Annabelle jumped down from her chair at the kitchen table and ran over to her mother. She buried her face into her hip, and hugged her around her waist.

"As a matter of fact, nigga, yes we do! So what the fuck you plan on doing about it?" Joaquin asked, as he stepped to him. They were standing one foot away from each other.

God put his hands together like he was about to say a prayer. Instead, he shut his eyes and bowed his head, taking a deep breath. Once he calmed himself down, he went ahead and addressed Joaquin like a mature man. "Look, bruh, I don't know what just went down here, but I'd appreciate it very much if you'd leave—now!"

Joaquin angled his head and looked at his ass like he was nuttier than squirrel shit. "Nigga, you got me fucked up, I'm not going a goddamn place! You got life fucked up!"

God frowned, and his nostrils flared. He wanted to split Joaquin's wig, but he was trying to maintain control of himself. He didn't want to cause a scene in front of Annabelle and scare her. "Look, my nigga, I'm asking you as politely as I can to—"

"Nigga, fuck you!" Joaquin shoved him hard, sending him stumbling backward. "I don't give a fuck how politely you're asking me to step off! Bottom line, I'm not going anywhere. So if you trying to get me to leave, then move me, fuck-boy!" He shoved him hard again. Abruptly, God took two swings at Joaquin but he ducked them with ease. Coming back up, Joaquin punched him in either side of his ribs and uppercut him. The blow sent God stumbling backward in a hurry. He flipped over the couch and landed on the coffee table, breaking it! He scrambled upon his feet, rubbing his aching head, groaning. When his eyes landed on Joaquin, he became enraged and charged after Joaquin, jumping over the couch. Joaquin swung on him, but he ducked his assault and grabbed him by his waist. He lifted Joaquin up effortlessly and slammed him down upon the table top. The legs of it exploded from underneath it, and splinters of wood went flying everywhere. Sitting on top of him, God started dropping punch after punch on Joaquin's face, bloodying his nose.

Joaquin held up his forearms and blocked his next couple of punches. He followed up by slamming his knee into God's crotch. He threw his head back, hollering loudly in excruciating pain and grabbing himself. Joaquin bit down hard on his bottom lip and kicked him square in the chest, sending him flying off of him. At this time, Billie and Annabelle were screaming and hollering for them to stop. Next, Charity walked inside the kitchen, rubbing her sleepy eye and wondering what was going on. She looked alive when she saw her daddy on the floor in agony. She grabbed one of the broken kitchen table legs to fend off Joaquin, but Billie snatched her back by her collar, making her drop the leg. She didn't want the little girl to get involved in the brawl and get badly hurt.

Billie knew she wasn't strong enough to stop two grown-ass men from scrapping, so she sent Annabelle to get her cell phone from her bedroom. Annabelle jetted out of the kitchen and returned shortly with her mother's cellular. Quickly, Billie dialed up her Uncle Kershawn.

"Unc, I need your help, get over here, now! This fool-ass baby daddy of mine and my fiancé are fighting! Yes! Joaquin and Kyree are throwing hands in the middle of the kitchen floor! Hurry!" Billie disconnected the call and stashed her cell phone inside her pocket. She watched as Joaquin and God circled one another, trading punches and jabs like professional fighters.

"No, daddy, stop, please, stop!" a crying Annabelle screamed aloud.

"Dad, no! Stop fighting! You can't fight 'em, he's Anna's dad!" Charity screamed aloud alongside Annabelle.

The girls tried to run over and stop their fathers from fighting, but Billie stopped them. She was fearful that something would go awfully wrong, in which case both of the girls would end up seriously hurt.

Please, Almighty God, let this end with both of these crazy men alive, Billie thought, as she held Annabelle and Charity at bay. The girls were struggling to break her hold, but she held fast.

God faked a left twice, and fired on Joaquin's mouth, busting and bloodying his grill. Joaquin took the punch like a champ. He tasted metal as the blood filled his mouth. He smiled amusingly and spat blood on the floor. God tried the same move again, but this time Joaquin avoided it and countered with two ribs shots. He followed up with an uppercut that nearly dropped God on his ass. The kingpin stumbled backwards and shook off his daze.

God and Joaquin went at it for a while. They went blow for blow until they both were exhausted and out of breath, breathing huskily, and pupils moving around aimlessly in their heads.

Realizing that he had to finish Joaquin off before he'd gotten his second wind, God threw a three punch combination at Joaquin—which he avoided. Joaquin came back in with a hook, which knocked sweat and blood from God, dropping him on one bending knee. God shook off the blow, looked up at Joaquin, scowled at him and rushed him.

"Ugh!" God tackled Joaquin and lifted him off his feet, carrying him and then slamming him onto the floor. He straddled him and rained punch after punch on his face. While he was taking the beating, Joaquin grabbed one of the bowls that had fallen to the floor. With all the strength he could muster, he slammed the bowl against the side of God's dome, exploding it.

God crashed to the surface, as broken shards of the clay bowl rained down upon the floor. God lay on the floor, wincing and dazed. Acknowledging that he had to get up before Joaquin could launch another attack, he scrambled to his feet nearly as fast as Joaquin did, reaching for the small of his back, for his gun. Joaquin turned around to face him, also reaching for the gun at the small of his back. Both of the men drew their guns, but Joaquin was just a little faster than God. As soon as God had extended his gun, Joaquin kicked it out of his hand and caught it. Scowling, Joaquin turned both of the guns on God and put him at his mercy.

"You were quick, but you weren't quick enough! Now, get on your fucking knees!" Joaquin roared. He had blood running out of his nose and over his lips, dripping to the floor. He was breathing heavily, and his hair was really frizzy from the brawl.

Mad-dogging Joaquin, God spat blood on the floor and said, "Fuck you!"

Joaquin fired a shot into the ceiling, and debris trickled to the floor. He then turned his gun back on God, yelling, "I said, *get cho black ass on your knees, nigga!*"

God took a deep breath and then got down on the floor, one knee at a time. "Good boy, now open your mouth for daddy!" God glared at him and clenched his jaws defiantly. "Either you do like I said, or I'ma murder you in front of your daughter. The choice is yours, big man."

God looked at a terrified Charity who was crying her eyes out. As much as he wanted to buck against Joaquin, he was going to do like he asked. His baby had already lost her mother. He didn't want her to lose him—her father! God looked at Joaquin and sighed, hesitantly opening his mouth. Joaquin smiled wickedly, having made him submit. He stuck his gun with the silencer on it so far down into God's throat it caused him to grimace and gag.

"Now suck on it!" Joaquin ordered, insanity dancing in his eyes.

God looked up at him hatefully. Enough was enough. There wasn't any way in hell he was going to give this crazy mothafucka's gun a blow job. "Nigga, fuck you, you just gon' have to kill me!" God said, barely audible, with a mouthful of gun metal.

Still smiling wickedly, Joaquin shrugged and said, "Okay."

"Please, please, please, no, don't kill 'em! Don't kill my daddy, Joaquin!" Charity pleaded for her father's life to be spared. She had tears sliding down her face and splashing on the floor. She and Annabelle were trying their best to break free of Billie's hold.

Annabelle finally broke free of her mother's hold and ran over to her father, hugging him around his waist. She looked up at him with pink, pleading eyes, tears spilling in buckets down her face. "Daddy, please, don't kill 'em, please! He's Charity's father! She's my best friend and my sister! Don't do it, daddy, don't do it! If you love me like you say you do, you won't kill 'em! Pleeeeeease!" she cried aloud and whimpered, holding her father's gaze as her bottom lip quivered.

Joaquin stared down at his daughter's face, and the hatred he had for God slowly melted away. He didn't know what it was, but it was something about his baby girl that made him vulnerable. In that moment, he wanted to pick her up, hug her, kiss her and tell her that everything was going to be okay. The anger he felt toward God didn't matter as much as the wants and needs of his darling Annabelle. Joaquin took an exasperated breath and looked at God. Although he wanted to blow his thoughts against the door of the oven, he was going to allow him to keep his life—for now. As far as he was concerned, there was always another day he could settle the score.

Joaquin eyed God menacingly. "You're lucky there's nothing I care more about than my princess, dick sucker. Otherwise, I wouldn't think twice about slumping yo' ass on this kitchen floor." Hissing, he stuck the gun he'd taken away from God into the front of his pants. He then eased his gun with the silencer on it out of God's grill, and scooped Annabelle up in his arms. She cried hard in his arms while he rubbed her back and kissed her on the side on her neck. "Papi is sorry, okay? I didn't want chu to see me behave like this, but I lost control and it led to this. Do you forgive me, baby? Do you forgive your papi?" Annabelle nodded. "I love you, princess. I love you so much. You're the best thing that I have in my life, and I never ever wanna be without you."

Charity ran over to God, and he scooped her up in his arms, comforting her. Billie ran over to him, and they had a group hug. God kissed both of his girls, then looked over at Joaquin. They glared at one another, with hostility pumping throughout their hearts. Joaquin mouthed to him *'This shit is far from over, watch your back'*, to which God replied *'Bet that. Watch your front'*. Joaquin nodded understandingly and pointed his gun with the silencer on it at him, making a gunshot sound with his mouth. He then smiled at him wickedly again, and tucked his gun at the small of his back. He yanked out his handkerchief and wiped the blood from his nose and the lower half of his face.

There was a rap at the door that made everyone prick up. Joaquin asked who it was, and then unlocked the door, pulling it open. He found Hugo standing before him with his gun at his side ready to pop something.

"What's up, Hugo?" Joaquin asked.

"Is everything okay? I saw silhouettes moving back and forth across the windows like people were fighting and then I heard shouting. I figured you were in trouble, so I hopped out of the car to see what wassup."

Joaquin smiled at the thought of Hugo having his back. He'd gotten the chance to chop it up with him while he was shopping, and it was safe to say that he liked him. He liked him a lot—in a manly way, of course. Joaquin patted Hugo on the cheek and then the shoulder.

"Everything is fine, my friend—relax," Joaquin told him.

Hugo stuck his gun inside the holster in his blazer. "Okay, I'd like to come in during the duration of your time here, if that's alright by you."

"Hey, if it's gonna make you feel better, knock yourself out, hermano." Joaquin opened the door further and stepped aside, allowing him in over the threshold. He introduced Hugo to Billie, Charity and God. They exchanged greetings.

Hugo looked at the mess the kitchen was in, and then at Joaquin questioningly. Joaquin smiled and shrugged.

"Family quarrel," Joaquin told him.

Hugo nodded and placed his hands on his hips, continuing to look over the mess inside the kitchen.

Joaquin went to shut the door, but stopped when he felt a hand upon it. Frowning, he opened the door back up and found Kershawn. He let him inside and closed the door shut behind him, locking it. As soon as Kershawn had seen Joaquin and God's battered faces, and then the mess inside of the kitchen, he came to the conclusion that they'd been fighting. Realizing that, Kershawn tucked his gun inside the holster in his suit's jacket. Billie greeted him and gave him a loving hug, and he kissed her on the cheek.

"You good, baby girl?" Kershawn asked with concern.

"Yeah, I'm fine. Thanks for dropping by."

"Don't mention it. You know you and Annabelle are my world."

Billie smiled when he said this. She liked the feeling of receiving a father's love from her uncle. Nothing would feel better beside the love of both of her biological parents. She wouldn't complain about that, though. She would be thankful for what she did have: a loving, caring, protecting and providing uncle/ father.

"Papi, can you tuck me in and read me a bedtime story?" Annabelle asked her father.

"Sure, princess," Joaquin told her. "Hugo, I'ma tuck her in and read her a story. Afterward, you and I can split." Hugo nodded and patted him on the shoulder. "Alright, lil' mama, off to bed we go."

"Gemme Charity—I'll put her to bed and clean up this mess while you clean yourself up," Billie told God and then took Charity—who was already falling back asleep—from him. Billie kissed him and went on about her business.

Kershawn and God chopped it up while Hugo busied himself on the sofa with a magazine. He was eavesdropping, trying to not to appear like he was paying them any attention. He ended up finding out about what had gone down between God and Joaquin.

"Anyway, Kershawn, lemme go up in here and wash up.

We'll rap later." God dapped him up and gave him a manly hug.

By this time, Billie had returned to the kitchen, sweeping up the broken shards of the clay bowl while engaging Kershawn in small talk. A while later, Joaquin emerged out of the hallway and motioned for Hugo to follow him. Hugo tossed the magazine he had been reading onto the coffee table and jumped to his feet, following Joaquin toward the front door.

"Billie, lemme holla at chu right quick," Joaquin told her, as he waited by the front door. Billie dumped the shards of the bowl inside of the trash can and walked over to see what Joaquin wanted. He grabbed her by the wrist and lifted up her arm, palm showing. He placed a bankroll with a rubber band tangled around it into her palm and closed it up. "That right there is for my lil' mama, make sure she gets everything she wants and needs with that." Billie nodded. Next, Joaquin leaned over extremely close to her ear so that only she could hear him, whispering: "I love you, and I always will. Don't chu every forget that." He kissed her gently on the cheek, then caressed the side of her face. He opened the front door, and Hugo walked out first. Joaquin looked back at Kershawn and waved. "Later, OG." Kershawn threw up his hand by way of saying goodbye. With that, Joaquin disappeared out of the apartment and shut the door behind him. Billie locked the front door and looked at the bankroll he'd given her. She stuffed it inside her pocket and went back to cleaning up the kitchen.

"I've got something I want to show y'all," God notified Billie and Kershawn, as he returned to the kitchen.

"What chu got?" Billie asked, having finished cleaning up the kitchen.

"It's inside of the bedroom, lemme show you." God motioned for her and Kershawn to follow him, as he turned around. They followed him inside the bedroom, where he plopped down on the bed and pulled open the top nightstand drawer. He took out a square black box and removed its lid, revealing five watches embedded in a bed of velvet. All five of the watches were digital, but three of them were black and made for adults. The other two were for children, little girls around Charity and Annabelle's ages. One was white and pink, with Minnie Mouse's face covering it. The other one was pink and had Daisy Duck's face covering it.

"Watches, huh? What are these? A late Christmas gift?" Kershawn asked, taking one of the digital watches that God passed him. He'd also passed one to Billie, who was sitting beside him on the bed.

"You could say that," God said. "I'd like to think of it as a necessity, though," he added and buckled the digital watch around his wrist, modeling it before his eyes.

"A necessity?" Billie's forehead wrinkled, wondering what he was talking about.

"Yes, baby." God kissed her on the cheek. "My baby is carrying my baby now. So we've gotta take precautions. You know what kinda business I'm in, and what kind of business your family is, and was involved, in." He glanced at Kershawn, who was an active contractor for several assassins. "You never know when or if the wolves are gonna be looking to snatch one of us up for a check or not. Should that happen, I'd feel comfortable knowing where you were taken so I could get you back."

God removed the placement that held the watches in it, and uncovered five sleek, black and metal location devices. God passed one each to Billie and Kershawn. Keeping one for himself, he extended the device's short antenna and explained to them how to use it.

"Pretty simple," Kershawn said as regards how to operate the location device. "Good idea, Kyree." He touched fists with God.

"Thanks, Kershawn."

Kershawn nodded in response. He then looked at his timepiece, his eyes widening, and he whistled. "Alright, folks, I've gotta be going. So, I'll get up with y'all tomorrow."

"Alright," Billie said, as Kershawn hugged and kissed her.

Kershawn shook up with God and patted him on his back, like all brothers do when they're greeting or about to part ways.

"I love you," Billie said, waving goodbye.

"I love you too," Kershawn said, as he followed God to the front door. "I'ma holla at Joaquin either tonight, or tomorrow sometime," he told God.

God held open the door, as Kershawn stepped over the threshold and turned around. "Kershawn, I appreciate you tryna straighten out what went down between homeboy and me. I really do. But with all due respect, I'ma handle that with 'em. I mean, I'ma grown-ass man and I'm not tryna come off like I'ma bitch or something—having my fiancé's uncle stepping into the middle of my beef like he's my father or some shit. Like I said, *no disrespect to you.*"

Kershawn nodded understandingly. "I feel you. Well, okay, I'll stay out of it, but should things get too funky, be sure to holla at me. 'Cause like I was saying earlier, we're family and I'm not tryna see things between y'all get bloody. 'Cause if it gets bloody, then it's gon' lead to deaths and if it leads to death, then it's gon' hurt Billie and those girls. And I for one cannot have that." He gave God a stern look. He was going to respect the boundaries that God had laid out for him, but if he felt he needed to step in, then that's exactly what he was going to do.

"Understood," God said, nodding.

"Smooth." Kershawn nodded.

"Goodnight," God said.

"Goodnight," Kershawn responded, walking away and answering his ringing cellular phone.

God shut and locked the door behind Kershawn. When he turned around, he found Billie standing behind him. She laid the side of her head against his chest and wrapped her arms around his waist. God kissed the top of her head and rubbed her back soothingly. He understood that what had gone down between him and Joaquin this night had mentally drained her. With that in mind, he wanted to comfort her and put her mind at ease. God knew that if he and Joaquin couldn't squash their differences, then eventually their quarrel was going to lead to an early grave for one of them. With that in mind, he was sure it was going to change Billie and the girls' lives forever.

God took a deep breath and continued rubbing Billie's back soothingly. He was a killa; there wasn't any doubting that. But when it came down to it, would he be able to crush his fiancée's baby daddy?

Fuck it! If it has to go there, then it has to go there—may The Realest Killa win, God thought, as he scooped Billie up into his arms and carried her off to their bedroom, where he planned to make passionate love to her.

Chapter 3

Joaquin was thoroughly impressed when he and Hugo arrived at Alvaro's estate, which was sitting on five hundred acres of land. The enormous grand mansion was eggshell white, and resembled a plantation house in the Deep South. It also had a silver twenty-foot-tall statue of Alvaro, which was dressed like an Aztec warrior, complete with helmet, shield, spear, and body armor. What Joaquin found comical was the fact that the statue of Alvaro was of a muscular build, when he was actually a short rotund Mexican man. The estate's lawn was well-manicured, and so were its rose bushes. Men dressed in black fatigues and carrying M-4 assault rifles patrolled the grounds with Doberman Pinschers on chain-linked leashes.

Hugo parked the limousine on the grayish black basalt paved driveway. He hopped out of the luxurious vehicle, closed the door behind him, and made his way around to the other side. He opened the back door and stood aside, allowing Joaquin to step out. Once he did, Hugo shut the door behind him and led him up the steps, to the big gray front door with a silver fist knocker on it. Hugo rapped on the front door; a moment later, it was opened. Alvaro's housekeeper, Bernadette, greeted them with a smile and stood aside. She was dressed in the traditional black and white maid's uniform, but what Joaquin found interesting was the strap of the machine gun she was wearing over her shoulder like a purse.

As soon as Joaquin and Hugo crossed the threshold inside the grand mansion, Bernadette shut the door behind them. Looking ahead, Joaquin and Hugo saw Alvaro zooming up the corridor toward them on a white electronic hover-board scooter with neon lights below it. Alvaro was going so fast that the end of his blue house robe ruffled at his back. A fat ass Cuban cigar was wedged between his chubby fingers, and he was taking pulls of it. He brought his scooter to an abrupt stop before his guests.

Alvaro was a balding man of a golden brown hue and a bushy mustache that curled over his top lip. He had a five o'clock shadow and a nest of grayish chest hair that led down his round belly. He was wearing boxer briefs and flip flops. Smiling, he stepped off of his scooter and approached Joaquin, giving him a manly hug.

"It's good to see you, amigo," Alvaro told him.

"It's good to see you too, hermano. Thanks for the shopping spree and the bag ya boy Hugo hit me with."

"Ahhh," Alvaro waved him off like it wasn't a big deal. "Don't mention it. That was peanuts."

"Yeah, to you, you rich fuck!" Joaquin laughed and threw phantom punches at him.

Alvaro laughed at him and threw his arm around his shoulders. "Hugo, take a load off and watch some television. Bernadette, see to it that the chef makes his favorite dish. You know what he likes."

"Yes, sir." Bernadette wandered off to do like she'd been told. Hugo removed his blazer and went to hang it up on the coat stand. He had it in his mind to watch ESPN and kick up his heels. He loved that big ass one-hundred-inch flat screen television inside the game room.

"I need a favor, Joaquin—I mean, a very big favor," Alvaro said, after taking the cigar out of his mouth and blowing out smoke.

"After the way you just looked out, whatever you've gotta ask of me, consider it done," Joaquin told Alvaro, as he led him down the hallway. At the end of the hallway, through the sliding glass doors, he could see people running back and forth across the backyard, laughing and playing around.

"I need someone taken care of, my friend," Alvaro said. "I want you to take a squadron of some of my most deadliest killaz and eradicate this pendejo."

"Who're we talking about, Alvaro?" Joaquin asked seriously. He knew Alvaro meant business by the expression on his face.

"Tomas. Tomas Salamanca."

"What's his beef?"

"You know, Joaquin, you never struck me as a nosy motherfucker."

"I'm not. But I'm notta toy soldier either. You can't just putta battery in my back, wind me up and expect me to go killing on command. I fuck witchu and all. But I've gotta know what I'm getting into here. You feel me?"

Alvaro nodded understandingly and said, "Yeah, I do."

Alvaro told Joaquin that Tomas was his cocaine plug. They'd fallen out a month prior, when Tomas had discovered that Alvaro had been having an affair with his wife. Tomas had murdered his wife, and had made two failed attempts to have him murdered. Now, Alvaro wanted to see to it that Tomas met his demise so he could go on living his life.

"I shoulda fucking known," Joaquin said. "There's always some broad at the middle of every war. Niggaz will send an army to kill behind some pussy in a minute, boy." He shook his head pitifully. He hated to be the one leading an army of killaz to their possible deaths behind some bitch. But he felt like he owed Alvaro for looking out for him. And he always repaid his debt. No matter what!

"So, what is your answer, yes or no? Don't keep an asshole in suspense," Alvaro told him.

They were now standing beside each other in the backyard—where pretty, blonde-haired white women in bikinis hung around the swimming pool. Some of them were splashing their feet around in the water; others were playing volleyball in the water, or horsing around. The only man present was a five-foot-eleven Mexican dude in navy blue, white and powder blue Polo swim trunks. He'd just scooped one of the white girls up from where she was lying in a beach chair sipping a Bahama Mama and flipping through the pages of a Vogue magazine. She hollered as he threw her into the pool. She quickly came back up to the surface, pissed off and dripping wet.

"Ricardo, you fucking douche bag!" the white girl called out to him, holding up her middle finger. He doubled over, laughing heartily with his hand on his stomach, slapping his leg. Afterwards, he climbed upon the diving board, ran forward, bounced off the end of it in a Cannonball position. His balled-up form came down hard, breaking the water's surface, and creating a big splash. Water went everywhere, coming so dangerously close to Joaquin he had to take a step back so he wouldn't get wet.

"You've been looking out for me since I touched American soil. You know I got chu. I can't turn you down."

Alvaro took the cigar out of his mouth and blew out a cloud of smoke, smiling. He was happy that Joaquin had agreed to take on the assignment.

"Thank you."

"No thanks needed."

"Okay. Well, name your price."

"Please, Alvaro, you don't have to gemme anything. I'ma do this on the love."

"Are you sure?"

"Yeah. I'd like to bring my man on with me, though. I'm sure you wouldn't mind blessing him with something."

"Are you vouching for this guy?"

"Most definitely am. We've been doing dirt together since I've been locked up."

"Okay, poppa, I'll give you a bag to give to him," Alvaro told him. "How do you feel about taking my nephew with you?"

"Who's your nephew?"

Alvaro nodded to whom the white girl had called 'Ricardo'. "He's been up here at the big house with me, smoking, drinking, eating and fucking these blonde bimbos like the world's gonna end soon." As Alvaro continued talking, Joaquin watched Ricardo in the swimming pool; he was in the middle of a three-way kiss with two of the pretty blondes. "He wants to be a part of the family business, so it's only right that he makes his bones. I needa see if he's cut out for the grunt work, then I'll let 'em move his way up through the ranks."

"Alright. Cool."

"I'll let chu meet 'em. Hold on." Alvaro snatched the cigar out of his mouth and called Ricardo. The young man looked over in his direction, and Alvaro motioned him over. "Come here, I've got someone here I want chu to meet."

"Ah, tio, I'm having fun with the girls, I'll meet your lil' friend later," Ricardo called out from the pool, with his arms hanging around the necks of the white girls. One was kissing up his neck while the other was sucking on his nipple.

Alvaro's face frowned up and he said, "Lil' Ricky, you get your brown ass outta the pool and over here now!" He jabbed downward with the hand he held his smoking cigar in. Turning to Joaquin, with teary eyes, shaking his head, Alvaro said: "I've kept him on a long leash since he's been here, on account of him losing his entire family. Tomas had his goons spray one of my cars that I'd gifted to my brother for his birthday. The limousine had tinted windows, so the hittaz couldn't see who was inside. They believed it was me though. Lil' Ricky's mother, father, and his kid sister were massacred." Alvaro loved his brother, his wife, and his little niece dearly. He blamed himself for what had happened to them. And he felt the only way to make things right was to ensure that Tomas never saw another sunrise again.

"Damn, I'm sorry to hear that," Joaquin said sadly.

"Hey, what are you gonna do? This is the life we chose," Alvaro said, then looked ahead. Ricardo was coming in their direction, dripping wet and leaving wet, bare foot impressions behind. He had a smile on his face as he adjusted his sliding trunks on his waistline. "Put some pep in your step, we don't have all day," Alvaro said.

"Joaquin, this is Lil' Ricky, my nephew. Lil' Ricky, this is a very dear friend of mine—Joaquin." Alvaro made the introductions with a smile. He had a hand each on their shoulders.

"What's up, man?" Joaquin extended his hand.

"What's up? You can just call me Rick or Ricardo." Ricardo shook Joaquin's hand. "I hate 'Lil' Ricky,' but I let my tio get away with it since he can't get over the fact that I'ma grown man now."

"You're barely eighteen. That's hardly grown."

"That's old enough be sent off to war and die for this country. So, in my eyes that makes me a grown ass man."

"Whatever, I'm not gonna argue witchu," Alvaro said, annoyed.

Alvaro then went on to tell Ricardo that he'd be busting a move with Joaquin and a few of his killaz to avenge his family. Ricardo's face took on a serious look then. He'd been waiting to get a piece of Tomas's ass since he found out he was the one behind the murder of his family. Since he'd been at Alvaro's mansion, he'd occupied his mind with sex and getting high, to keep from going insane over their deaths. But now that the time was at hand for him to get some payback for his loved ones, he was ready and willing.

"When are we supposed to make this move?" Joaquin asked.

"How does tonight sound? I've kept things quiet purposely for months to make him think I've tucked my tail and ran into hiding. But what I've actually been doing is my homework. I've managed to find where that cocksucker lays his head at night. If you hit 'em back, say, like, eleven o'clock tonight, he'll never see you coming. I mean, if you're up to it."

"If you want it done tonight, then we're moving tonight," Joaquin told him, pulling out his cellular phone. "I just needa hit my man up and let 'em know I'ma need his assistance."

"Okay." Alvaro nodded. "Well, once you wrap things up with your comrade, I'd like for you to upwind, get your polla sucked by any one of these bitchez and—You know what? Fuck it." Alvaro called over the prettiest white girls over in Spanish. Once she came over, he hung his arm around her shoulder and turned her to face Joaquin while he was talking on the phone. "This man right here is like my blood. You know what? Scratch that, he's my family. My hermano—so I want chu to take good care of him, chica. Suck his polla, lick his cojones, and fuck him 'til he goes blind. Okay?" The pretty white girl nodded. "Good girl." He smacked her on her ass and walked back off into the house.

Ricardo ran towards the pool and did another Cannonball dive into it, splashing water everywhere.

The pretty white girl pulled her wet hair back and tangled a thin band around it. She then unbuckled Joaquin's belt, unzipped his pants, and pulled them down around his ankles. She stroked his thick, vein-riddled dick with one hand until it was hard and curving to the left. She spat in her palm and used it to lube up Joaquin's piece, jerking it up and down. Next, the white girl massaged his slightly hairy nut sack in the palm of her delicate hand, and slobbered on his meat. Her ocean-blue eyes stared up at the blissful expression on his face, as she bobbed up and down his piece, spilling her hot saliva over his hanging sack.

"Y—Yeah, that's—that's the address—be—be here in like two—two hours," Joaquin stammered with his eyelids shut, enjoying the bomb ass head that was being bestowed upon him. "Nothing nigga, I'm good! Awww, fuck!" Joaquin's face frowned up. He held the top of the white girl's head, humping into her mouth. She started gagging and making slurping noises in between. "Yo', man, I'll holla at chu once you get here. I gotta go. Peace." He disconnected the call and tossed his cellular aside. Gripping either side of the pretty white girl's head, he stared down into her eyes and stroked her mouth passionately. You would have thought he was piping down her pussy. Looking ahead, he saw the young bull—Ricardo—fucking one of the white girls on a beach chair. One white girl was kissing the back of his neck while her tits were hanging out. The one that was getting fucked doggy-style by him from behind was eating the pussy of another.

Ricardo looked over at Joaquin and smiled, throwing his head back, like, *What's up?* Joaquin returned the gesture. He then pulled the white girl who was sucking his dick up to her feet. She sucked on his nipples while he fished through his pocket for one of the condoms Hugo had given him earlier. Once he found it, he tore open its golden foil wrapper and slid it down on his throbbing hard dick. Joaquin then forcibly turned the white girl around, bent her forward, and slid up in her from behind. Taking each one of her wrists, he brought her arms around her back and held her wrists down against her lower back.

Joaquin, frowning and biting down on his bottom lip, fucked the pretty white girl from the back savagely. Each one of his thrusts made her wet stringy hair bounce up and down, and she hollered out in pleasure. Her eyelids were shut, and her opened mouth displayed the gold stud tongue-ring at the end of her tongue. While Joaquin was wearing that ass out, he occasionally smacked her on her buttocks and left red hand impressions behind.

Once Joaquin and Ricardo's nut sacks were empty, they popped golden bottles of Ace of Spade, and snorted cocaine off the white girls' tits and ass. Joaquin and Ricardo chopped it up and got to know each other. It was during this interaction that Joaquin took a liking to the young man. The two of them just clicked. It was like they'd known each other all of their lives. Once Murtaugh arrived at the mansion, Alvaro came outside with a map that was the layout of Tomas's entire estate. Together, the men discussed how they were going to gain access to the mansion and launch their attack. Joaquin came up with an idea that they all agreed upon.

With the plan memorized, Alvaro rolled up the map and handed it to Joaquin. He then gave him the location to meet the killaz who were going to carry out the mission with him. Hugo drove Joaquin, Murtaugh and Ricardo to a disclosed location where they met the killaz. The men strapped up in body armor and camouflage fatigues. They then placed ear-buds inside the ear so they could communicate among one another. They sheathed bowie knives, then stacked them-selves up with arms and ammunition of their choice. After-wards, Joaquin went over the plan he'd formed earlier along with the others. Once he was assured everyone had mastered their roles in the mission, they boarded the airplane which was going to release them over the drop zone—Tomas Salamanca's mansion.

***

As usual, it was a quiet and boring night for the armed guards that patrolled Tomas's estate with their German shepherds. One guard in particular stopped on the side of the mansion, took one last drag from his cigarette and mashed it out under his black combat boot. He slipped the leash of his dog around his wrist and turned to the tall bushes, unzipping his cargo pants. The guard pulled out his flaccid meat and began to piss. He tilted his head back and sighed as he relieved his bladder.

The German shepherd had finished taking his leak before its master, and wiped its back paws on the grass. It started sniffing the ground until something had caught its eyes. Looking up into the sky, it saw several men hanging on parachutes gliding their way down to the ground. The German shepherd looked alarmed and began growling angrily.

"Woof, woof, woof, woof, woof!" The German shepherd barked loud and aggressively.

When the dog started barking, the guard hurriedly put up his dick and zipped up his cargo pants. He snatched up his M-16 assault rifle and ran over to the hound, standing upright beside him. He scanned the grounds for anything the dog could possibly be looking at as a threat to the estate's security. His face twisted angrily when he didn't see anyone or anything. Right then, one of the other guards came in over his walkie-talkie, asking about the happenings on his side of the mansion.

"Nah, everything is fine over here. It's just this goddamn dog." The guard spoke into the walkie-talkie. "I told you we needa getta younger one. This puta is so old and crazy he's seeing things."

"Woof, woof, woof, woof, woof!" The German shepherd barked louder and more aggressively. It then got into an attack stance and lowered its head, growling menacingly.

"Shut the fuck up, you stupid dog!" The angered guard kicked the German shepherd, and it whimpered.

Right then, four drones equipped with machine guns flew from around the corner. The guard narrowed his eyelids into slits and peered closely. He was trying to see what was coming at him in the dark.

"What the fuck!" the guard said disbelievingly. He didn't understand the flying objects flying at him. He'd never seen them before. He lifted his walkie-talkie to report to the other guards his sightings, but he was too slow in taking action.

Burrratatatatatatatatatatat!
Burrratatatatatatatatatatat!

The first wave of bullets from the drones blew out the guard's brains, knocking his plain black cap off his head. As his body collapsed to the ground, the drones kept firing at him, putting several more holes in his body.

"Woof, woof, woof, woof!" The German shepherd barked upward at the drones flying its way. It tried to jump into the air and snag one of them, but it missed. Right after, the rest of the drones gunned it down and kept on flying around to the other side of the mansion. The last of the guards had seen the drones coming at them, and they hoisted up their M-16s to open fire on them. Their German shepherds started barking loud and madly at the drones.

Burrratatatatatatatatatatat!
Burrratatatatatatatatatatat!
Burrratatatatatatatatatatat!
Burrratatatatatatatatatatat!

The guards managed to shoot down all of the drones right before them, but their dogs were sent to their bloody deaths. The last drone hurled downward, crashing and tumbling across the lawn. It bumped up against a booted foot, smoking full of holes. The booted foot belonged to none other than Joaquin who'd just made his way around the corner of the mansion. He had on a camouflage bandana tied around the lower half of his face, a tactical bullet-proof vest, and camouflage cargo pants. Two pistol-grip automatic shotguns were sheathed on his back to form an X. A machine gun was cradled in his gloved hands, and a bowie knife was sheathed on his hip.

Joaquin, looking at the opposite side of the mansion, made eye contact with Murtaugh, giving him a thumb up. Murtaugh's face was covered in green and black war-paint, and he was dressed in a tactical bullet-proof vest, camouflage cargo pants and combat boots as well. His muscular arms were riddled with veins and shone from perspiration. He clutched an AR-15 assault rifle at his shoulder. He gave Joaquin a thumb up as well, letting him know everything was copacetic on his side.

Joaquin nodded to him and looked over his shoulder at Ricardo, giving him the signal to do his part. Ricardo, who was dressed similar to him, ran from behind Joaquin with an explosive tucked under his arm. He attached the explosive to the double doors of the mansion. Kneeling, he punched a few buttons on the key pad of the explosive, and red digital numbers appeared on its display. The numbers rounded down, and Ricardo ran off to take cover.

Ka-boom!

There was a loud and furious explosion. Right after, fire and black smoke rushed out from the space where the doors once were. Joaquin gave his killaz the signal to follow him, before he went charging inside the mansion. They charged in right behind him. Together, they moved through the smoky foyer, and the small fires scattered throughout its floor. The infrared lasers of their machine guns shone back and forth across the mansion, as they moved their deadly weapons from side to side. With the assistance of the thermal readings of their digital headsets, they saw Tomas's armed goons running back and forth across them. Some of them were creeping along the upper level of the mansion, trying to see where they were, so they could pick them off. The other armed goons were on the ground level. They were at a disadvantage since they couldn't really see through the smoke wafting through the air. Their handicap would prove to be their undoing, though. Joaquin and his killaz were going to take full advantage of their disability.

The sound of rapid gunfire filled the air, along with the painful hollers and groans of death. Bullet-riddled bodies on both sides fell to their bloody demise and lay bleeding on the floor.

"Y'all head up to the upper level and see if you can find Tomas," Joaquin called out his orders while firing his machine gun, flat-lining goon after goon. "The rest of you, come with me! We'll seize the ground floor! If Tomas is here, we'll find 'em, and if we can't, I'll blow this fucking place to smithereens!"

"Alright, you guys come with me! Let's move, let's move, let's move!" Murtaugh told the men on either side of him.

Murtaugh hoisted up his AR-15 assault rifle and led his

killaz up the staircase, engaging the opposition in a firefight. More screams and hollers came as Tomas's goons were chopped down. Once Murtaugh, who was also second-in-command, had ran out of ammunition, he snatched the Dundee-style, eleven-inch bowie knife from where it was sheathed on his thigh.

"Come on, tough guy, let's see what chu got!" Murtaugh challenged, motioning for a goon to engage him in combat while he held up his bowie knife.

The killaz at his back went around him to make a clean sweep of the upper level of the mansion, leaving him to engage in a Game of Death. The goon Murtaugh was facing threw down his assault rifle and pulled a bowie knife equal to the size of his opponent's. He smiled devilishly and chuckled.

"I'm gonna gut chu like a fucking fish, chupapollas!" the goon told him, with every intention of making good on his claim.

Grunting, the goon took four swipes at Murtaugh, coming dangerously close to wounding him. Unfortunately for him, Murtaugh moved like the blowing wind. He tried to take a couple of swipes at the goon, but his attacks weren't successful. Swiftly, he jumped back when the goon thrust his knife forward. Countering, Murtaugh sliced him across his hand and severed the ligaments therein. The goon howled in pain, and Murtaugh kicked his kneecap inward, breaking it. Once the goon dropped down to one knee, Murtaugh stabbed him in his stomach and pulled the hilt upward. The goon's bloody intestines, spleen, and the rest of his insides spilled out onto the floor. His eyes bulged, and his mouth quivered. Gripping his bowie knife with both hands, Murtaugh slammed it into the top of the goon's skull, and then he violently snapped his neck. The goon fell face down on the floor. His blood ran out of him and dripped off the edge of the floor above, trickling to the floor below.

Murtaugh placed his boot on the head of the goon he'd murdered, pinning it to the floor. With two strong tugs, he yanked his knife out the top of his skull, wiped it on his pants leg and sheathed it where he'd pulled it from. Picking up his AR-15, he reloaded it and glanced over the railing. When he made eye contact with Joaquin, they saluted each other and joined their warring parties' hunt for Tomas.

Tranay Adams

Chapter 4

After he'd saluted Murtaugh, Joaquin led the rest of his killaz inside of the dining room, chopping down every goon they came across. Joaquin lost three of his killaz in the gun battle inside the dining room, which left him with Ricardo to back him up.

Joaquin and Ricardo threw down their empty machine guns at the same time. Joaquin reached over his shoulder and drew one of his automatic shotguns. Ricardo, on his part, pulled a Glock 19 from the holster at the small of his back. They placed their backs against each other and took in their surroundings. They listened closely to the gun battle going on upstairs. Shortly, armed goons stormed the dining room from both sides, spitting flames at them. The rapid gunfire shredded a family portrait hanging on the wall, blew a gazillion holes in the walls, sent splinters flying, shattered a flower vase, spilling water and roses. Even the wooden chairs surrounding the dining room table was chopped up into splinters.

Joaquin kicked one of the goons in the chest and then blew his head clean off his shoulders. He whipped around to his left and let the barrel of his shotgun erupt. A fireball flew out of it and made another goon do a back flip. While Joaquin was laying the goons down on his side, Ricardo was holding his own as well. He was quite the marksman with his aim, giving the goons on his end head-shots. The goons' heads snapped back, as their foreheads were impacted by bullets.

Their blood and brain fragments splattered against the walls, floors, and paintings on the walls.

Ricardo believed he'd dispatched all of his threats, but there was one left just barely alive. The goon winced in agony, as he sneakily gripped his M-16 and shot Ricardo's legs from under him. In free fall, Ricardo pulled a second gun from the holster under his arm. He pointed both of his handguns at the goon that had just blown out his legs, and pulled their triggers back to back, rapidly. The handguns spat fire at the goon and blew chunks of meat, bone, and skull out of his face. What was left of the goon's head dropped to the floor, and blood pooled around it.

"Shit!" Joaquin turned around to Ricardo with his smoking shotgun. He'd just laid down another goon moments prior.

Joaquin rushed over to Ricardo and kneeled down to him, taking stock of the damage done to him. The young man's legs were bloody and mangled, with broken bone sticking out of them.

"I got 'em—I—I got 'em, Joaquin—Didn't I? Didn't I—I—get 'em?" Ricardo said and then coughed up blood. Tears pooled in his eyes and ran out the corners of them.

"Yeah, you got 'em, Ricky, you got 'em good too, man. You blew his goddamn head off!" Joaquin replied, cosigning his comrade's kill.

"Pinche, puto, shoulda—shoulda known bet—better than to f—fuck with the fastest gun in the west, huh?" Rick said with a smile. Then, he started coughing again.

"Yeah, you were definitely fast, kid," Joaquin told him, cracking a smile. "Look, man, hang in there, save your energy—I'ma find Tomas's bitch-ass and we're gonna get chu outta here and to a hospital as soon as possible. Okay?"

"It's—It's far too late for me, poppy."

"Shut up, bro, don't talk like that," Joaquin chastised him. He saw that he was reaching for his hand, and he grasped it. "It's not too late. Just hang in there, you hear me? Hang in—" the rest of his words died in his mouth when

Ricardo moved the hand clutching his gun from his chest. He revealed two bloody holes in his chest. "I don't—I don't understand how this happened. You're wearing a bullet-proof vest."

Loud shouting stole Joaquin's attention. He scanned the dining room, waving his shotgun around at any threats that may be lurking in the shadows. Hearing the shouting again, Joaquin realized it was coming from upstairs. Murtaugh and his killaz were undoubtedly in a firefight with Tomas's goons. Shortly, there was a loud explosion that rocked the entire mansion like a 7.0 earthquake. The enormous crystal chandelier hanging from the ceiling, over the dining room table, rattled loudly and a crack formed across it.

Joaquin lowered his shotgun and focused his attention back on Ricardo. The dying young man told him that he'd been shot with armor-piercing rounds. That was how he'd been left in a bad way.

"Fuck, Ricky, man! Look, hang tight, you can beat this shit," Joaquin assured him. "You can—" Once again, Joaquin's words died in his mouth, hearing rapid gunfire coming from upstairs again. He looked up to the ceiling and hoped it wasn't his killaz that were on the losing end. "Ricky, I'ma—" Joaquin cut himself short when he saw that Ricardo was dead. His eyes were wide, and his lips were parted. Bowing his head, Joaquin said a quick prayer for him and kissed the gold rosary around his neck. He then, with a brush of his hand, shut Ricardo's eyelids.

Joaquin sat his shotgun upon the dining room table. He pulled out a vial of coke from his pocket, opened it, and tapped it. A small mountain of the white substance collected on his fist, and he snorted it up. He threw back his head and pinched his nose closed. He felt the urge to sneeze, but didn't want to waste the cocaine he'd just tooted up his nostril.

Bringing his head back down, Joaquin snorted up another small mountain of coke from his fist. He then capped the vial and shoved it into his pocket.

Joaquin's eyes were red webbed and glassy. His pupils were dilated, and green transparent snot was oozing out of his right nostril. Hearing hurried booted footsteps coming his way from the opposite direction, he knew it was the opposition, and that it was time for him to head back into the action. War-ready, Joaquin picked up his shotgun off the dining room table and pulled his other automatic shotgun from the holster on his back. He then ran into the hallway to continue the fight. He found three goons with M-16s coming at him blasting. Their bullets ate up the floor of the corridor and chopped up its walls. Debris sprayed from the walls, and dust clouds filled the air.

Bloom, bloom, bloom, bloom, bloom!

The barrels of the automatic shotguns jumped in Joaquin's gloved grips as they erupted, one after the other, and blew the goons apart. Their blood dotted the walls and floors of the corridor before they plummeted to their deaths. Joaquin was still standing with both of his automatic shotguns extended and wafting smoke, his chest rising and falling as he breathed. Seeing that he'd slain the goons successfully, he tossed the shotgun aside, knowing it was empty. Next, he reloaded the remaining one with the belt of shells hanging across his body.

Chick-chick!

Joaquin racked the shotgun and slowly made his way down the hallway, stepping over the dead bodies littering it. As he walked along, he heard something coming from one of the rooms, so he turned his head and listened closely. His face frowned up when he realized he recognized the voice of one of the two men talking. Upon listening further, he realized it was Alvaro's voice he was hearing. Now, the other man's voice he wasn't the slightest bit familiar with, but from the authority in it, he guessed it was a man in law enforcement.

"Listen, I can—I can give you ten million doll—" Alvaro was cut short by the law enforcement officer.

"I don't want your fucking money, you undocumented, Goya bean-eating, Mexican piece-of-shit!" the law enforcement officer shouted. "Don't you know that trying to bribe an officer is another offense? You're already looking at a kingpin charge! I guess you wanna keep adding to the list, huh?"

"No, no, no, I don't," Alvaro assured him, sounding defeated. "Okay, you wanna play ball then let's play ball."

Joaquin came out of the hallway and into a small foyer. There were movie posters on the walls, wax statues from iconic film characters, burgundy leather cushioned chairs, a small table; a burgundy and white popcorn machine, which was in the middle of making popcorn. Joaquin looked to the double doors at his right, next to the popcorn machine; the conversation was coming from there. He didn't know for sure, but he believed there was a movie theater beyond those twin doors.

"Smart, man, 'cause that's the only way you're gonna see your way outta this," the law enforcement officer said.

Joaquin switched hands with his automatic shotgun and tried to open one of the doors of the theater. When the doors wouldn't come open, he blasted apart its locks and forcefully kicked them, swinging them inward. The theater was dark. The only light was the one illuminating from its screen. Looking up, Joaquin took note of what was on it. It appeared to be Alvaro sitting down at a table inside an interrogation room. His left wrist was handcuffed to the table top, and a can of Pepsi set to the side of him. He was looking timid as a mothafucka, nothing like his usual arrogant and intimidating self.

Nah, Alvaro was very submissive. And Joaquin could see why. He was being drilled by a white man who was sitting on the table, looking at him, hands resting in his lap. The white man was obviously a detective, possibly in his mid-to-late forties. He was wearing a tie and button-down, with his sleeves rolled up. His shield was clipped to one side of his belt, while his gun was holstered on the other.

"Okay—I can give you some guys I know that are doing their thing in the streets," Alvaro told the detective.

"Hold on," the detective picked up the small notepad from the table top and snatched an ink pen out of his shirt pocket. He was ready to jot down everything he was about to be told. "I'm gonna need territories, names, associations and how much product they're moving. Now, before you decide to give me a line of bullshit, I want chu to know, I'll see to it that the number the judge hits you with will look like the digits on your social security card. You got that?"

"Yeah, yeah, man, I got it." Alvaro assured him, "No bullshit! If you'll be straight with me then I'll be straight with you."

Suddenly, the detective's cellular rang and he looked at its display. It was his wife. He answered it and told her he was in the middle of something and he'd get back with her. He then said, "I love you too. Bye." Once he put his cell phone away, the detective focused his attention back on Alvaro. "Alright, Alvaro, tell me something good—" he looked to him with the ball of his ink pen pressed to a sheet of the notepad.

The entire time the conversation between Alvaro and the detective was going on, Joaquin was standing in the isle of the theater, clutching his shotgun with both hands. His eyes were wide, and his mouth was hanging open in amazement. He was frozen solid. He couldn't believe what he was seeing and hearing. He was working for a fucking rat. The most low-down, dirtiest piece of godforsaken shit you could ever find yourself allied with. Joaquin was so fucked up behind what he was seeing on the screen that he'd forgotten what he was actually there for. It wasn't until the man he and his killaz were sent to kill spoke that he snapped out of his hypnotized state.

"Mr. Torres, I'm so glad you could finally make it. You're a little late for the show, but you most definitely walked in on the best part," Tomas told him from where he was seated at the middle of the theater. His back was to Joaquin, and he was eating from a big bucket of popcorn. He hadn't bothered to turn around to address his guest. It was as if he wasn't concerned with Joaquin being there to kill him. It was just another day for him.

At that moment, Murtaugh and the rest of the killaz, machine guns up, slowly entered the theater, swaying their weapons around, their UV-lights and infrared lasers cutting through the darkness.

"Is that him? Is that Tomas?" Murtaugh asked, approaching at Joaquin's rear, ready to obliterate the drug lord alongside his comrades.

"Yeah, that's him," Joaquin confirmed, without turning around to him. Murtaugh and the killaz moved to gun down Tomas, but Joaquin threw up his hand and told them to fall back. "Look up at the screen and pay very close attention," he told Murtaugh. Reluctantly, Murtaugh and the killaz lowered their machine guns and looked up at the theater's screen. They were shocked and disappointed as well, gaining the knowledge of Alvaro's secret.

"I know it was Alvaro who sent you here to kill me, my friend. Lemme guess, he gave you some shit about him nailing some broad of mine as the reason I want to kill him? Yes, it's true. He did bang a chica I had on my arm, but so fucking what! I change up women like I change my fucking draws. A man of my status never goes to war for the sake of pussy—ever! We go to war because of family, honor, and the almighty American dollar, my friend." Tomas relaxed in his seat with his back to them, like he wasn't worried about getting his head blown off. "As for the truth of why I want him dead, well, you've just seen it play out—right before your very eyes."

Right then, Tomas sat his bucket of popcorn down on the seat beside him. Rising to his feet, he brushed the crumbs of the popcorn from off him and stepped out into the aisle, with a pistol-grip AK-47 attached to two drums. He was dressed in a cream-colored linen suit which he wore a Kevlar bullet-proof vest over. He had a very thick graying beard, and shoulder-length hair that he had pulled back in a bun. Casually, he strolled up to Joaquin and his killaz, assuring them that he didn't pose a threat to them, holding one of his hands up.

"Okay, Alvaro's a filthy fucking rat, so now what? What do you think we should do?" Joaquin scowled at Tomas and gritted, nostrils flaring.

"Take his place," Tomas told him. "I know your background, so I know you're cut out for it."

"How do you know anything about me?"

"Mr. Torres, I make it my business to know any and everyone associated with my—quote unquote—*business partners*," Tomas told him. "It not only keeps me abreast about situations like the one playing out before your eyes on the screen behind me, but it keeps me in the know about the individuals I am dealing with. You see, in this business you'll find you have no friends and no one, absolutely no one, is to be trusted. Any more questions, Mr. Torres?"

"Yeah, what do you mean by take his place?"

"I supplied that fat bastard with so much coca he could ski on it," Tomas said. "I can give you kilos for the same price I was giving him. You can pick up from where that cheese-eating fuck left off and make a fortune. Or—" he opened his arms and looked at the surrounding balconies. The lights of the theater popped on one after another. Joaquin, Murtaugh and the killaz looked up at the balconies where Tomas was looking. There were goons upon them with AK-47s pointed at them, from either side. Right after those goons had appeared, the ones on the grounds of the theater appeared. Rows and rows of them popped up from behind the theater seats and pointed their AK-47s at them. Looking around, Joaquin and his comrades knew they didn't stand a snowball's chance in hell in against Tomas's army. So the offer he laid on the table for Joaquin was looking like a damn good one. "—We could blow you off the face of the fucking planet. The choice is yours, negrito." Tomas's face balled up angrily when he said this. He was dead-ass serious too. He and his goons would gun down the opposition if they decided to buck. He didn't give a mad-ass fuck about any of them. They could either get down or lay down. It didn't make any difference to him.

***

The next day

Alvaro had gotten the confirmation of Tomas's assassination in the wee hours of the morning. He made sure

Murtaugh had gotten his quota for his participation in the mission, and still dropped a bag on Joaquin. Now he was seated at his favorite diner, having one of his favorite meals. Afterwards, he planned on catching a matinee at the closest AMC Theater, which was only a couple of blocks from the establishment.

Alvaro sat at the window of the diner, in a booth, enjoying his meal of medium rare steak, peas, and mashed potatoes, surrounded by his goons. Alvaro's head bowed as his fork and knife went to work, cutting up his juicy porterhouse, which was running with hot juices. While the kingpin partook in his meal, the waitress walked back over with a burgundy cup filled with fruit punch. She sat the cup down on Alvaro's table, and turned to walk away. She'd taken two steps when one of the goons smacked her on her ass, causing her to stop. She wanted to curse his ass out and smack fire from him, but she didn't want to cause a disturbance and lose her job.

The entrée bell hanging over the door rang, as an old African American man came through it. He looked to be in his late seventies, wearing a black fedora and midnight blue suit. He walked like the hunch back of Notre Dame, with the assistance of a cane. The waitress that had just left Alvaro's table asked if he needed help, but he waved her off, insisting he was fine.

"You sure, sir?" the waitress asked, concerned. The old man looked like he was having trouble walking and would tip over any minute.

"No! Young lady, I told you I was fine!" the old man snapped at her rudely. Her eyes bulged and she held up her hand, letting him understand she didn't want any trouble. She then went back to wiping the down counter top like she was doing before he'd walked into the diner.

The old man sat down on the stool at the counter and leaned his cane against it. He then removed his fedora and sat it down on the counter top, picking up the diner's menu. He looked over the menu, trying to decide what he'd like to eat. Making up his mind, he motioned the waitress over and told her what he'd like. As she listened to him, she jotted down his order on a small notepad while chewing gum.

"Okay, coming right up," the waitress told him. She was about to walk away, but he grabbed her wrist and slipped something inside her hand. Her brows furrowed. She wondered what he'd given her, but she didn't bother asking him once he gave her a stern look.

The waitress poured the old man a cup of coffee and sat it down in front of him. He pulled the metal container over to him that housed all of the packets he'd need to fix his cup of coffee to his liking. Sipping his cup of coffee, he looked up and saw the waitress talking to the big, burly cook. The big man's forehead wrinkled, as he listened to what the waitress had to say. When she pointed at the old African American man, the cook looked back and forth between them, while holding what she'd given him in his meaty hand.

A moment later, the cook and the waitress made their way out of the kitchen and out of the door. The bell hanging over the door rang as they took their exit, signaling the attention of Alvaro and his goons. They exchanged glances, wondering what the fuck was going on. Just then, a youthful Native American man came through the back door, making the bell hanging above it ring. Alvaro and his goons looked behind them; they made a move to draw their guns, but the Native American cat already had the drop on them. His black leather-gloved hands lifted up a handgun with a silencer on it. With precision, he shot two of the goons through the forehead, and they dropped where they stood. Seeing Hugo about to draw his gun as well, the Native American man swung his handgun around to him. Instantly, Hugo lifted his head up and held his hands up, surrendering. The Native American approached him and removed his gun from inside of his jacket. Holding Hugo at gunpoint, he ejected the magazine from the bottom of the gun and threw the gun into the kitchen.

Right then, there was a click sound as the front door was being locked. Everyone looked to find the old African American man locking the front door and turning the sign over to the 'Closed' side. He drew the blinds over the door and slowly made his way over to the windows of the diner, twisting the small stick at the ends of them, to shut them. Only until then, did the old African American man stand upright and let his cane fall to the floor. He pulled out a pair of black leather gloves, slid them over his hands, and pulled a handgun with a silencer from the small of his back. It was already cocked, locked and ready to kill anyone it was pointed at.

The old man made his way toward Alvaro, who looked fearful. He had food at the corner of his mouth and stains from the steak on the cloth tucked inside his shirt. His head whipped back and forth between the Native American man and the old African American man, wondering what was about to go down.

"Wait—Wait a minute! What's—What's going on here?" Alvaro said in a squeaky, panicky voice.

"What's going on here is the execution of a fucking rat!" the old African American man told him. He was now standing at his table with his gun at his side. His voice sounded very familiar to Alvaro. His brows furrowed, trying to put his finger on the face it belonged to. He was sure it wasn't of the man standing before him, because they didn't even match.

"Joa—Joaquin, is—is that you?" Alvaro asked. Joaquin didn't say shit. "What—What the fuck are you talk—talking about, man? I'm notta rat!"

"So you say." Joaquin pulled his cell phone out of his pocket and played the recording of Alvaro giving information inside the interrogation room. Alvaro was scared as shit. He didn't know how the hell Joaquin had gotten his hands on the recording, but he knew for sure there was no way he was making it out of that café alive.

Alvaro found himself in a desperate situation, one he was willing to do anything to get out of. Alvaro slid out of the booth and got down on his knees, crawling over to Joaquin on his hands and knees. He hugged Joaquin's leg and pleaded for his life, teary eyed.

"Please, please, poppy, don't kill me! Please!" Alvaro begged, tears streaming down his cheeks. "I—I'm sorry, okay? Look, I can give you money. How about twenty million dollars—cash? I can—I can give it to you right now. All I have to do its make a phone call and I'll—I'll have it."

Joaquin looked up at the Native American man, who was actually Murtaugh; he didn't say anything, so Joaquin focused his attention back on Alvaro's pitiful ass. "For real? Twenty million—cash?"

"Yes. All I have to do is make the phone call, you'll get the deniro and I'll be on the next flight outta L.A. I swear to God, Joaquin, on my mother's grave." Alvaro looked up at him with his hands together, pleadingly.

Joaquin stood, there looking down at Alvaro for a while. He was scowling and silent, thinking about the kingpin's offer. Suddenly, he clenched his jaws and kicked Alvaro in the mouth, launching his head backward. Alvaro fell back against the floor, bleeding at the mouth and looking at

Joaquin confusingly. He touched his lip, and his fingertips came away bloody.

"Fuck you think I am, Alvaro? You think a man of my caliber can be bought? Huh?" Joaquin shouted at him. "Allowing you to live would be a slap in the face of every street nigga alive or dead! I've done a lotta wicked shit in my lifetime that I've gotta live with, but letting you breathe another day won't be one of them." (*Joder, crees que lo soy, Álvaro? Crees que un hombre de mi calibre se puede comprar? Eh? Permitir que vivas sería una bofetada en la cara de cada negro callejero vivo o muerto. He hecho muchas cosas malvadas en la vida con las que tengo que vivir, pero dejarte respirar otro día no será una de ellas.*)

Upon hearing Joaquin's response, Alvaro's eyes grew bigger and his mouth flung open. He watched in horror as Joaquin tucked his gun at the small of his back and placed his leg on the seat of the booth. Pulling up his pants leg, he revealed a sheathed bowie knife, which was strapped around his calf. Joaquin unbuckled the sheath and drew his bowie knife.

"This is gonna get messy," Joaquin said to no one in particular. He then addressed Hugo. "Big man, hold this nigga down!"

Alvaro screamed, hollered and even pissed his pants, as he struggled against Hugo. Still, his attempt to stop from being restrained was useless. Hugo managed to pin Alvaro's wrists to the floor. He continued to scream and kick, but Joaquin straddled him. Joaquin grabbed Alvaro by the lower half of his face and squeezed so hard his mouth came open. Swiftly, Joaquin grabbed hold of his slimy tongue and brought his bowie knife toward it.

"Since you love to flap that big ass fucking tongue of yours, I'm gonna cut it right out of your goddamn mouth!

You cheese-eating, cabrón!" Joaquin said angrily. He pulled Alvaro's tongue further out of his mouth, making him scream louder and kick harder. Slowly, Joaquin began to cut Alvaro's tongue out of his mouth, blood dotting his face. The more of the kingpin's tongue he cut, the more his blood dotted his face. Finally, Alvaro's tongue came loose and Joaquin looked at it. After tossing the severed tongue aside, Joaquin stood upright and wiped the blood from his face with the back of his gloved hand. Looking up at Hugo, who'd also gotten blood on him, he turned the bowie knife around so he'd be holding its blade. Extending the bowie knife toward Hugo, he said, "Gone and finish him off, big homie."

Hugo narrowed his eyelids at Joaquin, wondering if he had some kind of trick up his sleeve. He wasn't moving fast enough, so Murtaugh pressed his handgun against the back of his head. Feeling the gun's silencer pressed against the back of his dome made Hugo make up his mind quickly. He took the bowie knife from Joaquin, pushed Alvaro forward so he'd be sitting up. Hugo then snaked the hand, holding the knife around his neck. Alvaro's eyes were hooded, and he was bleeding profusely from his mouth. His face was sweaty and pale. He'd lost so much blood that he didn't have any more fight left in him. Hugo was basically about to perform a mercy killing for the poor bastard.

Hugo glanced up at Joaquin, who gave him an approving nod. With the permission granted, Hugo dragged the bowie knife from one side of Alvaro's neck to the other, slicing his jugular. Buckets upon buckets of blood spilled from out of the wound Hugo created. Alvaro went limp, and Hugo allowed his lifeless form to smack back against the floor. Standing upright, Hugo looked at Joaquin—with both his hands and knife dripping blood. Joaquin plucked the handkerchief from out of his jacket's pocket and unfolded it, extending it toward Hugo.

"Go ahead and place it into this handkerchief, big homie," Joaquin told him. Hugo did like he was told and used a nearby napkin to wipe off his bloody hands. "This was a blood pact. By doing this you have agreed to keep your mouth shut about—this." Joaquin looked around at the dead bodies bleeding out on the floor. With that said, he wrapped the bloody knife neatly and headed toward the back door of the diner, alongside Murtaugh.

Murtaugh tucked his handgun at the small of his back. He unlocked the door and pulled it open. He and Joaquin were about to walk out, when Hugo said something else that stalled them.

"Seeing that I'm unemployed now, I'm gonna needa job," Hugo said, stepping toward them. "I was thinking, maybe, I'd come work for you."

Joaquin and Murtaugh exchanged glances. Joaquin looked back at Hugo, smirking. He'd always liked the hulking Mexican since he first met him. He was a cool ass nigga, despite him being a straight up goon. This was why he'd spared his life in the first place.

Chapter 5

God posted up outside, smoking a blunt and watching the Mexicans lather his SUV. He was so engrossed with what was going on with his truck that he didn't even notice someone approaching him from behind until the person was standing beside him, trying to light up a half smoked blunt of his own.

"Damn, this mothafucking lighter ain't worth a shit; I shoulda got myself a Bic," Joaquin complained and threw the cheap lighter across the way. He then turned to God and said, "You gotta light, my nigga?"

God stood there staring at Joaquin like he was crazy. They were beefing, so he was surprised he was speaking to him. He was expecting him to come up behind him and blow his fucking head off, so this was quite a shock for him.

God gathered himself and said, "Yeah, I've gotta light." He fished his lighter out of his jeans and took the liberty to fire up Joaquin's blunt. He watched as he took a few puffs and blew out a cloud of smoke. In the midst of him doing this, God eased his hand toward the blower in the small of his back. A smirk formed at the corner of Joaquin's lips. It was like he already knew what God was up to. God's forehead wrinkled, finding this odd. Right then, he saw a shadow moving up behind him. He moved to react, but it was already too late.

Crack!

A masked goon cracked God upside his head with a retractable baton, causing him to double over. A second masked goon came from the side of him and hit him in the back of the kneecap with a retractable baton, bending him down to one knee. A third goon, wearing a black ski mask over his face, busted him in the arm and the ribs with his

63

retractable baton. A van screeched to a halt in front of God, and the door swung open. God, wincing from the pain inflicted on his body, rushed the goon that had pulled open the van's door, punching him. The blow connected and laid his ass out inside of the van, leaving his legs hanging out of the van.

God then turned around and fired on another one of the goons, dropping him. He then kicked another one in the balls, and once he doubled over, he kicked him square in the face. He fell backwards onto the ground. God went to rush the last goon, but the goon that he knocked back inside of the van, grabbed him in a chokehold. He then pulled his ass inside of the van. The rest of the goons piled up inside the van and pulled the door shut. The van drove off, with the goons beating the living shit out of him.

Meanwhile, another masked goon, at gunpoint, backed the Mexicans up from God's truck. He jumped into the SUV, fired it up, and sped out of the car wash parking lot. Right after, a black on black Tahoe truck with Joaquin onboard pulled out of the lot and drove off in the other direction, leaving the staff of the car wash looking around dumbfound-ed.

***

The goons that had kidnapped God continued to kick, stomp, and whack him with their retractable batons. His face was battered, bruised, swollen horrifically and bloody. He was sure one of his bones was broken, and he was finding it harder and harder to breathe. All of the fight had been beaten out of him, so all he could do was lie there while the goons continued to assault him.

Once the goons had grown tired of working God over,

Aztec, who was one of the goons rocking a ski mask, shoved them away from him. He spat a thick glob of mucus in God's face, as he lay moaning in pain. He then threw his retractable baton aside and pulled out his blower, cocking a hollow-tip round into its head. He leveled the gun at God's dome piece and was about to pull the trigger, when he was interrupted by the ringing of his cellular. Pulling out his cell phone, he looked at its screen, seeing 'Big Bro', which was the name he'd programmed Joaquin under in his contacts.

Aztec pulled his ski mask above his eyebrows and answered the call, placing his cell phone to his ear. He listened to what Joaquin had to say and hated what he was hearing. Still, he respected his street brother as acting boss; so he'd abide by his orders.

"Alright, bro, just so you know, I'm not feeling this shit, but you're the jefe so I'ma roll with it. Okay, hermano, peace." Aztec disconnected the call and stashed his cell phone in his pocket.

"What did he say?" one of the goons asked.

"Yeah, what did he say?" another one of the goons inquired curiously.

"To let this worm off the hook!" Aztec's voice went up an octave when he said 'hook', and kicked God in his side. God howled in pain, wincing and turning over onto his side, holding it. "I was just about to send you to your heavenly kingdom, but my hermano—the merciful mothafucka that he is—decided to let chu keep your life," Aztec regretfully informed him before kneeling down to him. "He said to tell you to thank my niece—Annabelle. She begged him to spare your sorry ass. If you know Joaquin, there's no one in this world that he loves more than baby girl. He didn't have it in him to break her lil' heart." He took his gun by its barrel and whacked God upside the head, knocking him out cold.

"Are we still dropping this mothfucka off to be cremated, man?" the goon driving the van asked.

"Nah, change of plans, dog—we're dumping this piece of shit at the hospital," Aztec told him.

"Alright, hospital it is," the driver replied.

***

Skirrrrrt!

The van skidded to a stop outside the emergency unit, and its side door slid open. The goons threw God out onto the pavement, a few feet away from the double doors of the emergency unit. A second later, God's truck skirted to an abrupt stop beside the van he was transported in, and the goon driving it hopped out. Hurriedly, he ran around the truck and climbed inside of the van, pulling the sliding door closed. Right after, the van took off in a hurry.

God, with slimy bloody strings of saliva hanging from his bottom lip, slowly got upon his feet, wincing. Holding his aching side, he limped toward the emergency unit's double doors, teetering between consciousness and unconsciousness. As he made his way across the waiting room lobby of the emergency unit, he garnered the concerned stares of those waiting to be seen. Finally reaching the front desk, he dinged the metal ringer on the counter top for the nurse's attention. When she arrived at the window, she looked to be annoyed until she saw his battered and bloody state.

"I—I—I needa—I needa, uhhh—" God's words trailed off. His eyes rolled into the back of his head, and he fell backward, banging the back of his head off the waxed floor.

***

Billie emerged from the elevator, holding Charity and Annabelle's hand. She was walking so fast that the girls were having trouble keeping up with her.

"Mommy, slow down, I almost fell," a frowning Annabelle complained.

"Yeah, you're moving too fast for us to keep up," Charity said, nearly tripping and falling.

"I'm sorry, girls, I'm just in a hurry to make sure Kyree is okay," Billie replied, as she walked down the hallway, looking on either side of her for God's hospital room. "This is it," she announced, seeing the number on the side of the door. As soon as she and the girls walked inside, they saw Kyree lying up in his bed. The self-proclaimed God of the Streets was battered, bruised and swollen. His head was wrapped in bandages, his nose was in a splint, his jaw was wired shut, and his left arm was in a cast. His right eye was slightly swollen shut, and his left one had blood clots in them.

Three men surrounded God's bed. They were discussing getting revenge for the brutal beating he'd gotten. The first man on the left side of her fiancé's bed was five-foot-eleven, with big untamed hair. He had hideous scars on his face that he'd gotten from makeshift shanks while in Youth Authority, and missing knuckles he'd gotten from the many brawls he'd been involved in—in and out of correction facilities. To his family he was known as Jayion, but the streets knew him as Buck Wild.

The hulking, two hundred and something odd pounds of muscle, standing on the opposite side of the bed, was his cousin—Big Country. Country was a dark chocolate brother with a mouth full of shiny gold teeth. He wore his hair in deep waves faded on the sides, and had a goatee that aligned his mouth to perfection. Country was a wildling that hailed from a notoriously violent neighborhood called Overtown in Miami, Florida. Murder was his game. His involvement with two homicides back home made him lay low on the West Coast. One night out on the town with the boys eventually led to him bearing arms. Impressed by his talents with a gun, God made him an offer to join his organization that he couldn't refuse.

The young man at the foot of God's bed went by the name Asad. He stood five-foot-ten and weighed a total of one hundred and seventy-five pounds, which was all muscle. He was a fairly attractive youth who'd taken to wearing his hair in a nappy Mohawk. His bulging pecks and ripped arms tested the limitations of the black Balenciaga T-shirt he was wearing. He had diamond earrings hanging in both of his earlobes, and a thick gold rope chain around his neck. A lion's head medallion the size of a saucer hung from the chain. 'Asad' is Arabic for 'lion', which was his reason behind purchasing the piece of jewelry. Besides being one of his top shottas, Asad was someone God held in very high regard.

Spotting Billie and the girls at the door, Country looked to God and then nodded to them. God looked over at his fiancée and his daughters, and a smile formed on his lips.

"Y'all gemme a minute with my family, man," God said, as Billie approached with the girls.

Billie gave all the men a sisterly hug before they greeted the girls on their way out of God's room.

"Hey, Uncle Asad—hey, Uncle Buck—hey, Uncle Country," Charity said with a smile, as she waved at her play uncles. She then gave them all a hug and a kiss each on their cheek. Annabelle followed behind her, doing the same.

"Daddyyyy!" Charity ran over to her father's bedside and hugged him. Wincing, he leaned over and hugged her with his good arm and kissed her on the lips.

"Hey, baby girl, daddy missed you," God said to his daughter, sounding muffled with the wire holding his jaws shut.

"I missed you, too." Charity frowned, as she gently touched her father's battered face. She then looked to his casted arm and wondered what had happened to him. "What happened to you? Are you all right?" she questioned with concern.

"I'm fine, lil' mama. I fell off the back of my friend's motorcycle, is all."

"You've gotta be more careful, daddy. If I lost you I woulda been so sad." With tears in her eyes, Charity hugged her dad again. He held her tight with one arm and kissed her again, rubbing her back comfortingly.

"What's wrong with your mouth, da—I mean, Kyree? Why do you sound like that?" Annabelle inquired with creases on her forehead. She was checking him out from head to toe, taking in the stock of the injuries he'd acquired.

"They had to wire my jaws shut 'cause I'd broken them in the motorcycle accident," God told her.

Annabelle climbed up in his bed along with Charity. Together, they kissed God all over his face to make his 'boo boos' feel better. They then hugged him.

"Y'all smile and hug 'em again. I'ma take pictures of you all." Billie smiled as she snapped pictures of the girls and God with her iPhone. She then lay across him and they took pictures as a family as well.

"I needa talk to you," Billie whispered in his ear and rose from off the bed.

"Okay. Do the girls have their ear-buds so they can listen to music?" God asked, as he caressed Charity's cheek with the back of his hand. She smiled at him and kissed his palm.

"I got mine!" Annabelle said, as she held up her ear-buds and iPod.

"Good," Billie said and kissed her baby girl on the cheek. "How 'bout you, lil' lady?" she addressed Charity about her ear-buds and iPod.

"Yep," Charity replied, putting in her ear-buds.

"Hey, how 'bout you girls listen to music and draw daddy a picture on his cast and sign it, huh? How is that?" God said, looking from Charity to Annabelle.

"Yay!" Charity and Annabelle said in unison, clapping their hands. With that response, Billie grabbed two black Sharpie markers from out of her purse and passed one each to the girls. Once Charity and Annabelle started drawing on God's cast, Billie turned the volume up on their iPods as loud as they could stand them. She then plopped down in the chair and focused her attention on God, maintaining eye contact with him.

"What happened? And don't gemme any bullshit about you falling off the back of someone's motorcycle either. 'Cause we both know you're too macho to be riding on the back of some nigga's motorcycle and holding on to 'em like some bitch." Billie's tone was damn serious.

God grinned and said, through his wired jaws, "Well, damn, that's how you greet your man? No *how're you doing baby*, or *I love you* or nothing? Damn, ma! You're as cold as a pimp's heart!"

"I'm sorry, baby," Billie presented him with a fake smile as she leaned forth, then caressed the side of his face. She kissed him and continued to caress his face. "I love you. How're you feeling?"

"Okay—you can knock it off now," God said as he looked at her like she was doing too much.

"Hey, you asked for it." Billie lay back against the chair how she was before and crossed her legs. She nestled her hands in her lap and looked at God. "Now, tell me what really happened."

God's face suddenly took on a serious expression. He took a breath before giving his sweetheart the rundown. When he finished with what he had to say, Billie's expression didn't change at all. She didn't seem the slightest bit surprised at what Joaquin had done. In fact, she was more surprised that he hadn't followed through with just killing him. She didn't know what it was that stopped him from making sure her man was dead, but she was honestly happy that he hadn't.

"You don't seem the least bit surprised by any of this," God said, as he wondered why his wife-to-be didn't even flinch about what he'd told her.

"I'm not," Billie told him. "To keep it one hundred witchu, Joaquin is a dangerous man; a very, very dangerous man. While you and I grew up in the hood, he grew up in a place as close as hell as you can get without dying. He had been conditioned to not feel remorse or sympathy for any one short of myself and his daughter. In fact, if I hadda guess, the reason why he probably didn't follow through with your execution is on the account of how *pretty girl* feels about you." She referred to her and Joaquin's daughter, Annabelle. Upon mentioning her daughter, God looked at Annabelle who was side by side with Charity, drawing on his cast. They appeared not to have a care in the world besides listening to their music and doodling on him. The sight brought a grin to his lips, and he looked back to Billie.

"Yeah, I'm sure it's 'cause of lil' mama that I'm alive today. "If he feels about Annabelle the way I feel about Charity then I know fa sho' that's why the nigga didn't murk me. Believe me when I say there is absolutely nothing I wouldn't do for my baby girl."

"Yeah, that's the same way that Joaquin is about pretty girl." Billie nodded. "So, where do you go from here?"

"You lemme worry about that," God said as he placed his hand on her thigh. "As for right now, I wanna get married." '

"Well, I've been looking and—"

"Nah, you not hearing me, ma." God shook his head, cutting what she had to say short. "I'm not tryna wait. I'm tryna get married, like, *today*. Not tomorrow, or the next day after but today."

Billie sat up in her chair with a frown. She didn't know if he was serious or not. "Are you serious right now? I mean, I do wanna marry you, but how're we gonna make this happen on such a short notice?"

"I'm sure I could arrange that." A voice came from the doorway.

God and Billie looked to find Kershawn leaning against the doorway. His arms were folded across his chest, and his legs were crossed at the knee. He was wearing a black turtle neck and a light-gray suit with black plaid print. This getup, accompanied by his glasses and modest Movado timepiece, made him look like he'd walked off the set of a photo shoot for a GQ magazine feature.

"Hey, look, it's Uncle Kershawn!" Charity announced, as she pointed to the ex-hitman in the doorway.

"Uncle Kershawn!" Annabelle's eyes widened surprisingly. She and Charity dashed over to him, and he scooped them up in his arms. He smiled as they kissed him on either side of his cheek. "How'd you get here?"

"My chauffeur, pretty girl," Kershawn answered.

"You mean, Humphrey?" Charity asked.

"Yep," Kershawn replied, looking to her. "He's downstairs waiting for me now."

Lipton Humphrey was a forty-something white British man with citizenship in the United Kingdom and the United States. He was handy with a gun and quite an asset behind the wheel of a car. One particularly was Kershawn's 2021 black Rolls Royce Phantom. His job was: getting his boss to where he needed to be and making sure he got there safely. Everyone that came into contact with Humphrey loved him. He was a very likable man with an alluring accent, charming personality, a one million dollar smile and enough wit to unarm a bank robber. Now, don't get it fucked up, Lipton's easy going persona was on the surface; beneath it all lurked a beast that would devour any pour soul foolish enough to cross him. If you were his friend, then there wasn't anything he wouldn't do for you, but if you were his enemy—well, let's just say you'd regret the day you ever found yourself as such.

"Either I'm getting too old, or y'all are growing up and getting heavy. Lemme sit y'all down before this back of mine goes out." Kershawn sat Charity and Annabelle down on the floor. He then kneeled down to them, reaching inside his jacket. "I've got something for you two beautiful lil' sisters."

"For real? What do you have?" Charity asked excitedly.

"Yeah, what do you have? Don't keep an asshole in suspense!" Annabelle said. As soon as she realized what she'd said, her eyes bulged and she smacked her hand over her mouth.

Billie's eyes bulged, and God had the same reaction; their mouths flew open. They exchanged glances. They couldn't believe the mouth on Annabelle's little ass. They chuckled a little, but Billie knew she had to get serious and get on her daughter. She didn't want her thinking it was cool for her to become unruly at the mouth. Billie understood that if you gave a child a foot, they'd try to take a mile. And she couldn't have that. Nah, she was going to make sure she was raising an upstanding young lady.

"Pretty girl!" Billie scowled and shouted, stomping her foot. A scared Annabelle glanced back at her momma while fidgeting with her bottom lip. "You know better than to use that kinda language. What I tell you about that? Now, say sorry to your uncle—now!"

Sad, Annabelle turned to Kershawn and apologized to him. Her voice was small and weak, but he definitely understood her.

Kershawn smiled and said, "It's okay, pretty girl, it was just a slip of the tongue. We've all made mistakes. Come here," he pulled her closer to him by her little hand and kissed her tenderly on the forehead. "Now, you wanna see what I've got the two of you?" The girls smiled and clapped their hands, jumping up and down, excitedly. "Okay." Swiftly, he pulled out two long stem red roses from the inside of his jacket, passing one to Charity and the other to Annabelle. Instantly, the girls shut their eyes and inhaled the scent of the beautiful flowers.

"Oh, I love it," Annabelle said. "Thank you very much, Uncle Kershawn," she added, hugging him with one arm and kissing his cheek.

Charity switched hands with the rose, saying: "I love mine too. Thank you, uncle." She hugged him with one arm and pressed her cheek against his, lovingly.

Seeing their girls interact with Kershawn really warmed Billie and God's hearts. They enjoyed seeing their families acting so well together. It made them feel like their future together was going to survive the test of time.

Kershawn stood upright and placed his hands on Charity and Annabelle's back, guiding them toward God's bedside. The girls followed his lead, as they continued to inhale the scent of their lovely red roses. "Now, as far as that wedding goes, I know someone that can make that happen onna spot. All we've gotta do is get chu two into the right kinda threads, if you know what I mean. Are y'all ready?" He looked from Billie to God, smiling.

God, looking up into Billie's eyes, caressed her hand with his thumb as he held it. "Oh, I'm definitely ready. How about chu, ma? You ready to spend the rest of your life witta nigga?" he asked with a smile.

"All of this life and the next," Billie replied, leaning down and kissing him.

Kershawn smiled and rubbed his hands together in anticipation. "Good. Lemme make a phone call. What time is it?" With a flick and thrust of his wrist, he glanced at his exalted timepiece. Right after, he pulled out his cellular and speed dialed a Holy Man that had a direct line to the Lord himself. The man in question picked up on the third ring. "Hello, Minister Franklin? This is Kershawn. Look here, I know it's beena while since we've chopped it up, but I needa favor. You think you can make it down here to UCLA Hospital in say, uh," he glanced at his timepiece again. "Three hours?"

Chapter 6

Three hours later

Billie and God's wedding hour had finally arrived. It took place inside God's hospital room; on the day she had come to visit him. Now most people couldn't afford to arrange a wedding on such a short notice, but God was handling a little paper, so he was able to pull it off. They'd agreed to have something small with just Kershawn and the girls as guests. Later in the year they'd planned to have an epic ceremony somewhere in Barbados, where they'd invite both of their families.

Billie and God weren't religious, but they did believe in a higher power. Still, they didn't belong to any church; so they didn't know any ministers they could get to marry them. That's where Kershawn came in. Old Uncle Kershawn knew a lot of people with various trades that were indebted to him in one way or another. So when he found out that his adopted daughter needed someone to marry her and her fiancée, he didn't waste any time getting in contact with Minister Johnny Franklin. Minister Johnny Franklin was a smooth talking pimp turned Man of God. He drove a line of luxury vehicles that estimated a total of five million dollars. The mansion he and his wife lived in was rumored to be three-point-one million dollars. And that was just one of the properties he owned.

Minister Franklin ran a mega church as big as Yankee stadium. He had arguably one hundred thousand members that attended his house of worship Tuesdays, Wednesdays, Thursdays and Sundays. There were whispers of Minister Franklin's net worth being an estimated thirty million dollars. With the number of members his church had and the government not taxing churches, Kershawn wasn't surprised with the fortune he'd amassed. Kershawn looked at religion as being one hell of a hustle. It made him wish he'd picked up a Bible long before he picked up a gun.

Minister Franklin had fallen indebted with Kershawn on account of him being extorted by a couple of wise guys. When he had gotten the call for him to step in on his behalf, Kershawn made an example of one of the Made Man and promised to do even worse to his family if he and his goons continued to harass Minister Franklin. After Kershawn had laid his gangsta down, Minister Franklin didn't have any more trouble with the mafia. It came at a price though: one hundred thousand dollars in cash and a lifetime debt to Kershawn.

As far as Minister Franklin was concerned, he'd gotten off easy. He could have ended up chained to a bolder at the bottom of the ocean, with eels and other creepy sea creatures swimming in and out of his nose and mouth.

Billie and God stood facing each other, smiling. They both were glowing and happy to finally be taking the necessary steps to spend the rest of their lives together. Billie was absolutely stunning this day. Her face was beat and her auburn hair was laid to the Gods. The diamond earrings hanging from her earlobes resembled small crystal chandeliers, and the diamond-studded necklace decorating her neck looked like the piece that sunk with the Titanic. She wore a platinum and diamond tiara around her head. Her shapely body conformed to the fitting white dress which boasted her impressive cleavage and her teardrop ass. Billie's dress, which Charity and Annabelle had assisted her in picking out, was worth five thousand dollars. It was a V neck sweep, brush train lace tulle, long sleeve, sexy see-through number with embroidery cascading ruffles.

It had taken some effort, but God had gotten out of bed and on his feet. He'd be damned if he got married to the woman of his dreams while lying down. Kershawn had placed a call to his personal barber, a dark-skinned Belizean cat by the name of Mervin. He arrived at the hospital within an hour and cleaned up God real nice. He had him looking like a million bucks in all crispy one hundred dollar bills. When Mervin held the mirror up to God so he could get a good look at himself, he couldn't stop smiling at his reflection.

Once Mervin was paid and sent away, God jumped into the shower and got dressed in his underwear. By the time he'd come out of the bathroom, the suit and shoes he'd ordered from the Neiman Marcus magazine was waiting for him. God unzipped the black bag his attire came in, and he couldn't stop smiling. Enclosed was a light-gray slim, fitting suit, matching button-up vest, button-down white shirt and baby blue tie.

After God had gotten dressed, Kershawn assisted him with securing his tie around his neck and tying it. He put on the titanium Rolex timepiece Billie had got him for the occasion. He completed the ensemble with his light gray slip-in dress shoes. To top it off, he sprayed Christian Dior's *Sauvage* for men on his neck and the inside of his wrists. He then turned to the girls, asking them how he looked. They told him, "You look handsome, daddy." He then hugged and kissed them, waiting for his bride-to-be to enter the room.

The bright sun shone through the wall-to-wall glass window and caused everyone inside God's room to appear like they were glowing. Minister Johnny Franklin stood on the side of them. He was a five-foot-eleven heavy-set man of a brown hue, and he had a graying beard. The fat of his neck hung over the collar of his powder blue button-down shirt.

He was wearing a striped navy blue suit and leather, and suede slip-in dress shoes. Minister Johnny Franklin had been sweating profusely since his arrival, so he kept his handkerchief in his hand to tend to it.

"Billie, when we first met, I never imagined this day would come, but now that we are here I couldn't have imagined choosing anyone else but you to spend the rest of my life with. You're the most beautiful woman in the universe. There are so many things about you that I love. But if I were to run—" God became teary eyed and his voice cracked emotionally. He took the necessary time to gather himself before continuing with what he had to say. "If I were to run down everything I love about you we'd be here for an eternity—" He sniffled. Tears slid down his cheeks. He looked at Kershawn. He was holding Annabelle in one arm while his other arm was hung around Charity's neck. Though Kershawn was smiling, Charity and Annabelle's noses were red. They were crying. God couldn't help smiling, seeing both of his daughters were caught up in one of the most important days of his life. "—So, I'll tell you just a few things I love about you," God took a deep breath before continuing. "I love how you make a cute snort when you laugh, I love that incredible, breathtaking smile of yours and I love your loving and caring nature. I promise to support you and our girls for the rest of our lives. You all will never want or need anything for as long as I live. I promise to honor you and to love you unconditionally, even when we're hot at each other. Billie, I can't imagine where I would be without you, and I cannot wait to continue this crazy journey with you by my side. I love you in this life, the next and our last."

After reciting his vows, God pulled out his handkerchief and dabbed his cheeks dry. He then he dabbed the wetness from Billie's cheeks and tucked his handkerchief back inside the breast pocket of his suit's jacket.

Billie's eyes were pink and wet from her crying. Sniffling, she went on to recite her vows but her voice cracked emotionally. Fist to her mouth, she took the time to clear her throat before going on to say what was in her heart.

"Kyree, I was drawn to you from the day we met. Your warm and inviting eyes, your handsome face, and your sexy smile softened my rough and rugged façade expeditiously. I remember wanting to have, and sometimes make, reasons to talk to you. To see you beam that astonishing smile back at me, immediately putting me at ease and brightening my day. Some people may think that we moved too fast with our special union, but to me the timing was perfect—for the both of us. You truly saw me. You understand me, accept me, in a way no one else has, in a way that I believe no one else can. You are my homie, my lover, and my best friend—" Billie's voice cracked emotionally again. She bowed her head as tears coated her cheeks. Taking a deep breath, she pulled herself together and looked back up at God. He pulled out his handkerchief again and dabbed her cheeks dry. "I'm so grateful to have you. I must say that you and the girls are an integral part of my life—" Charity and Annabelle exchanged smiles and interlocked their fingers. "You and I have a special, profound, unfettered love for each other. What makes it so unique is that we love each other at our most intimate, vulnerable and difficult times." Billie swallowed the spit in her throat before continuing. "I promise to love you always and forever—unconditionally."

Once God and Billie exchanged their vows, the minister then blessed them, joined their hands together, and asked, "Do you Kyree take Billie as your lawful wife, to have and to hold, from this day forward, for better or for worse, for richer or for poorer, in sickness and in health, to love and cherish until death do you part?"

"I do," God responded happily, smiling.

It was hot as fuck in the hospital, so the minister used his handkerchief to pat the beads of sweat from his shiny bald head. He then cleared his throat before continuing, focusing his attention on Billie, asking, "Do you Billie take Kyree as your lawful husband, to have and to hold, from this day forward, for better or for worse, for richer or for poorer, in sickness and in health, to love and cherish until death do you part?"

"I do," Billie answered happily, smiling.

After God and Billie had said, "I do," to the vows, Kershawn—the best man—gave the bride's ring to the minister, who blessed it and handed it to God to place on the Billie's finger. Then, Annabelle, who was the maid of honor, handed the groom's ring to the minister, who blessed it and handed it to the bride to place on the groom's finger. They each said these words, "I take this ring as a sign of my love and faithfulness in the name of the Father, the Son, and the Holy Spirit."

"Ladies and gentlemen, I now present to you, Mr. and Mrs. Kyree Purdy." The minister smiled proudly and patted the beads of sweat from his bald head again. "Kyree, you may kiss the bride."

God kissed Billie, and their family applauded them.

Billie turned to her Uncle Kershawn, flashing her platinum wedding band, mimicking Shug Avery from The Color Purple movie, saying, "I's married now."

Kershawn, God, Charity and Annabelle laughed heartedly, recalling the movie. Kershawn hugged Billie and kissed her on the forehead. They exchanged 'I love you's' before hugging once again. Reaching inside of his suit's jacket,

Kershawn pulled out a fat ass envelope and handed it to Billie. She peeked inside of it and saw that it was stuffed with crisp blue face one hundred dollar bills. She smiled broadly and looked up at her uncle, hugging him with one arm.

"Just a lil' something, something to get chu started out there in the world," Kershawn said with the side of his face pressed against Billie's, as she held him in a hug.

"Thanks, dad—I mean, Uncle Kershawn," Billie said. "I'm sorry; I didn't mean to—"

Kershawn grinned and said, "It's okay. I don't mind. Thought I'd never hear that from anyone in my life, seeing how I don't have any children of my own."

"No," Billie said, smiling. "You've always hadda daughter and a granddaughter." She scooped Annabelle up in her arms. "Isn't that right, pretty girl?"

"Yep," Annabelle cosigned. She hugged Kershawn around his neck and kissed him on the cheek. The old man blushed and grinned.

God scooped up Charity in his arms and kissed her on the cheek. Kershawn approached him and placed a hand on his shoulder, looking him in his eyes seriously.

"My girls are under your care now, so I expect you to take care of them. Not just financially, but spiritually, emotionally and physically as well." Kershawn spoke sternly. "Should you need any help—I mean, any help at all, in either of those departments—do not hesitate to give me a call. We're family now, and family looks out for each other." Kershawn extended his hand. God looked down at his hand and then back up at him, smirking. He shook his hand. Kershawn flashed him a smile and patted him on his shoulder.

***

Asad was creative in his approach to getting in the complex he needed to take his shot from. He'd gotten disguised as a homeless man, wearing a burgundy beanie, a beat up rusty-brown blazer, a charcoal gray blanket around his shoulders, and tattered baggy jeans which he held around his waist with a rope. He went unnoticed as he pushed his shopping cart among the droves of people, collecting recyclables, while they were busy having a good time at the shindig.

Once Asad made his way inside of an alley, he scanned the area to make sure there wasn't a soul watching him. Seeing that there wasn't, he rifled through the junk piled up inside of his shopping cart, until he found what he was looking for. A tool box that housed a host of items he'd need for his assignment.

Asad took another scan of the area before he approached the back door of the apartment complex. Noticing the cameras watching him attentively, he reached inside the recesses of his blanket and pulled out a can of black spray paint. He shook the can up and sprayed the lens of the cameras. He twisted the knob of the back door but discovered it was locked. Kneeling down to it, he sat his can of spray paint down on one side and his tool box on the other. He popped the locks on the tool box and revealed an assortment of items. He had pistols, silencers, suppressors, ammunition, grenades, smoke bombs, detachable scopes, etc.

Asad pulled on a pair of black leather gloves and took out the items he'd need to gain access to the back door. Once he was done picking the lock, he placed his items back inside the tool box and pulled out a Nighthawk AAC Recon. He then took out a matching silencer and screwed it onto the end of the Nighthawk's barrel. Squeezing one of his eyelids shut, his face frowned up as he took aim at imaginary objects to test the weapons sighting. Satisfied, Asad stood upright and opened the back door, pressing his back against it. He took the time to ready himself for the task ahead of him. Holding his silenced gun up at his shoulder, he took a deep breath.

"Alright, Asad, this is it, the point of no return," Asad told himself before entering the building.

Life is crazy as fuck, bro. Just to think not long ago God was 'bouta splash a young nigga. You fast forward to now, and that nigga is like a brother to me. And here I am now, about to guarantee one of his enemies a closed casket on his behalf.

Tool box held at his side, Asad opened the door of the stairwell and made his way up the staircase. Creeping his way up the steps as quietly as he could, Asad took headshots and eliminated the goons holding machine guns, acting as watchdogs for the festivities. Once he'd cleared the staircase, he went halfway back down them and entered a door that led to the twelfth floor. He made his way down the hallway, looking for the perfect residence for him to perform his task.

"And here's the lucky lady." Asad cracked a one sided smile. He then went on to pick the lock of the unit and opened its door. Once he'd gained access, he looked for the bedroom that was perfect for him to set up shop. He found it within a little boy's bedroom, which had blue decorations and toys scattered on the floor. Looking up, Asad spotted the bedroom's only window. He made his way over to the window, stepping over the toys scattered on the floor. Peering out of the curtains, he found that he had the perfect vantage point to take his shot from.

Asad sat his tool box down and whipped open his blanket, revealing a MPA 338BA Bolt Action Rifle, which had been hanging around his neck. He took the strap from around his neck, opened the sliding window, and sat a chair in front of it. Once he sat down, he removed the attachments he'd need for the rifle from his tool box. He attached the durable high-definition scope onto the MPA 338BA and screwed a suppressor onto its barrel. Next, he draped the blanket over him and his weapon so he wouldn't be so easily seen.

Sitting behind the powerful rifle, Asad placed a strip of gum inside his mouth and began chewing it. Through the lens of the scope, he searched the area for the man he'd been sent to kill—Joaquin Torres.

***

It was eighty-five degrees outside, with the occasional gust of wind. The fine-ass women with hourglass shapes were wearing bikinis, crop tops, Daisy Dukes, and next to nothing. They were either hugged up with their D-boy boyfriends, or the balling-ass nigga that was sponsoring them. If it wasn't that, then they were trying to garner the attention of the brother with top dog status, or the one that was next up to being the man. They and everyone else were watching the basketball game while enjoying ice-cold refreshments and popsicles.

Hugo, Murtaugh and Aztec were posted on the sideline with everyone else, watching the basketball game, which Joaquin was playing in. Aztec was one of the newer members of their organization; he had gotten out of prison a few days ago. Joaquin and he had known each other since he'd come to Los Angeles. In fact, he used to run the streets tough with his big brother, Psycho, until he'd gotten murdered in a botched robbery of a crack house. Ever since then Aztec, or Tec—which was what niggaz called him for short—had been under Joaquin. He treated him like a younger brother, making sure he was straight while he was locked up and when he came home.

Aztec was a five-foot-four, tan-complexioned Mexican with a shaven head. His short stature was covered in sculpted, bulging muscles. He had tattoos starting from his neck and stopping at his wrists. His ink was a billboard for his gang affiliation and his idolization of the Eagle Knights. The Eagle Knights—sometimes called Eagle Warriors—were a special class of infantry soldiers in the Aztec army, constituting one of the two leading military Special Forces orders in Aztec society. Aztec's family supposedly had the blood of some of those Eagle Knights coursing through their veins— which was why he'd taken up the name Aztec.

Although Aztec was only twenty-five years old, he already had OG status and respect on every prison yard he'd occupied. He earned his stripes in the streets for the barbaric levels of violence he meted out to those that wronged him and his loved ones.

***

"Fuck you crying for, ol' bitch-ass nigga? You signed up for some gangsta shit, right? Right? You hear me talking to yo' punk ass?" Aztec barked, and spit flew from off his lips. He stood on the side of a younger gangbanger from the wrong side of the tracks. He lifted his hand high above his head and smacked the shit out the back of his head, launching it forward.

The younger gangbanger was a Mexican kid that went by the name Infrared. He was crying like a little bitch, and green snot bubbles were coming out of his nose, oozing over his top lip. He was wearing a red bandana around his head and a Hawks jersey. A noose was secured around his neck and handcuffs kept his wrists bound behind his back. His legs were shaking crazily and occasionally buckling. A dark wet spot expanded at the crotch of his red Dickie shorts, and piss ran down his leg, creating a yellow puddle around his right Chuck Taylor Converse.

"P—P—Please, T—Tec, man, please, I—" Infrared was silenced when Aztec smacked the shit out of him again. His eyelids were shut and his mouth was trembling, as tears continued to stream down his cheeks. Infrared was shaking like he was a stripper at Magic City.

"Detén todas esas quejas y quejas, ese! (Stop all of that bitching and whining, ese!)" Aztec shook his head, looking at Infrared pitifully. He was glad that he wasn't one of his homeboys. He would have been a shame to see the way he was performing under the circumstances. The grown-ass man standing before him wasn't a G at all. "Seeing how much of a ho-ass nigga you are, I know yo' dead homies are turning over in their graves right now. And yo' big homies? Shiiiiiit, I know they'd be shaking their heads if they could see you right now."

"Dog, you don't have to—"

"Cállate! Cállate la boca! (Shut up! Shut the fuck up!)" Aztec snarled heatedly and balled his fist. He then kicked Infrared in his side and punched him in the mouth, bloodying his grill. Infrared winced and spat blood on the rooftop. The swift blow had nearly dropped him, but he'd managed to recover his balance. "You're notta gangsta, homie! Youz a mothafucking fraud, Vato, a perpetrating ass bitch!" Abruptly, he whacked him upside the back of his skull with his Beretta. The assault opened a bloody gash he'd definitely need staples to close up. Infrared's eyes rolled into the back of his head. He was about to fall off the rooftop, but he

regained control of his equilibrium. Looking down at the streets below, Infrared became dizzy seeing he was fifty feet from the ground.

I shoulda never raped that lil' bitch, dog! And I wouldn't have if I woulda known it was his niece, Infrared thought as he continued to shake all over, scared that he may lose his life.

Infrared made the mistake of putting Spanish Fly inside of Aztec's fourteen-year-old niece Maria's drink at a party. Once she was at his mercy, he took full advantage of her, raping her and sodomizing her. When Maria realized what was happening, it was already too late and she was too out of it to put up a fight. After Infrared had finished violating her, he returned to the party like he hadn't just raped a teenage girl in the other room.

Thinking about how foul Infrared had done Maria had gotten Aztec's heart pumping full of rage. He tucked his Beretta at the small of his back and kicked Infrared in his behind, sending him hurling off the rooftop. He screamed in terror as he plummeted toward the streets below. The length of rope around his neck quickly unraveled before straightening completely. The rope snatched Infrared back up and he swayed from side to side, dancing on the end of it. His face turned red, and veins bulged all over his bald head and neck. Blood clots formed in the whites of his eyes, and they became glassy. Shortly thereafter, tears spilled over the brims of his eyes and slid down his cheeks. Standing up above, Aztec watched with an evil smile as Infrared's bitch-ass continued to dance at the end of the rope. He eventually went still. His Chuck Taylor Converse slipped off his right foot and plummeted toward the ground, disappearing into the traffic below.

***

Aztec's eyes were hidden behind black sunglasses to shield him from the sunlight. He wore a wife beater, blue Dickie shorts and matching Nike Cortez sneakers. A white towel lay over his right shoulder; every now and again he'd use it to wipe his sweaty face with. Him, Hugo and Murtaugh were strapped up in case any drama popped off. Not only were they watching the basketball game, they were keeping an eye on everyone in the audience.

While they were on the ground, playing close attention to the people watching the game, the goons that Joaquin hired were posted up in an apartment building across the street, keeping their eyes on everyone in attendance. They were young street niggaz who Hugo had personally recruited himself. Joaquin had paid them a stack apiece for eight hours of work and another stack if they had to stay a couple of hours over. He figured it would be in his best interest to keep them around since he had bad blood with God.

Earlier that day, Joaquin, Aztec, Hugo and Murtaugh were playing a game of one-on-one basketball. They were only playing half court since a few other guys were running a game on the opposite end. One of the guys on the opposite end, by the name of Mekhi, had a crazy jump shot he swore no one could fuck with. Homie was popping mad shit on the court, and every shot he put up he sunk in the basket.

Joaquin and the rest of his crew, while taking a water break on the sidelines, watched Mekhi and his homeboys run their game. Joaquin could tell by the icy platinum chain he'd tucked into his shirt, the AP Rolex watch he'd stashed inside of his Nike duffle bag, and the MV Agusta F4CC, which was a motorcycle with a $120,000 dollar price-tag, that he was handling a little paper. With that in mind, Joaquin decided he'd seen enough of Mekhi's game out on the court and wanted to see how he'd do up against him.

While the young nigga was in the middle of talking shit, Joaquin jumped to his Air Jordan 13's and challenged him and his crew to a ten-thousand-dollar basketball game. Mekhi, not one to back down, accepted Joaquin's challenge. So here they were, the next day, with ten big ones on the line, running a game with a team of their choosing.

Joaquin and his team were slaughtering Mekhi and his boys. The score was twenty-seven to ten. Now, Mekhi had started the game with his usual bravado and showing off his skills with the basketball. But when Joaquin and his boys started digging in his ass, he became short with his team members and threatened them with violence. Joaquin smiled and shook his head, and his team continued to whip their asses.

Joaquin hit a three point jumper and hustled back up the court, laughing and smiling. Mekhi darted up the court and caught up with him, guarding him. While he was sticking him, Joaquin taunted him by talking in his ear.

"Looks like that ten gees is mine, homeboy," Joaquin said, smiling. There was sweat rolling down the side of his face. His shoulders and arms shone from perspiration. His bare upper body boasted his muscles and tattoos. The Air Jordan 23 basketball shorts hung slightly off his ass, showing the waistband of his Ethika boxer briefs.

A scowling Mekhi replied: "I wouldn't get too happy. It ain't over to the fat lady sings, my nigga." The ends of his thin locs were dyed royal blue and held back in a band the same color. His forehead, neck and shoulders shone from sweat. The tank top he was in had sweat stains at the back of it. He was wearing royal blue Reebok basketball shorts and the throwback white and royal blue Iverson sneakers.

"Somebody get Lizzo's fat ass on the phone, please!" Joaquin called out for everyone to hear him. Just then, one of Mekhi's team mates had launched the basketball in his direction. Seeing an opportunity to steal the ball, Joaquin jumped up and snagged the basketball from out of the air. He raced down the court with it, bouncing it fast and zeroing in on the basket.

"Shit!" Mekhi cussed angrily after Joaquin had picked the basketball out of the air. He knew he was about to score again, and that shit made him hot as crack cooking on top of the stove.

What had started out as a basketball game between two opposing teams, turned into a competition between Joaquin and Mekhi. They started hogging the ball and trying to outdo each other, displaying bad sportsmanship among their teammates. On the sidelines, Aztec was no longer paying attention to the basketball game. He, Hugo and Murtaugh were watching the four suspicious looking men on the other side of the court. They stood out among the rest of the spectators since they were the only men not there with women, or trying to holler at any of them. Aztec picked up that their sole focus was on Joaquin the entire time they'd been there. On top of that, they were dressed in black hoodies and had black shades covering their eyes. Aztec, Hugo and Murtaugh discussed this among themselves and found this odd. It was hot as a bitch outside, so why in the fuck were these fools dressed so warm! They had to have been packing heat. That was the only excuse for them to be dressed as they were.

Aztec said to Hugo, without taking his eyes off the men in the hoodies and shades: "Yo', dog, watch these fools. They're giving me funny vibes." Discretely, he picked up his hoodie, which his shotgun was concealed inside of. He wanted his piece nearby because he had a weird feeling that something was about to pop off.

"Yeah, they're giving me funny vibes too," Hugo replied while keeping his eyes on the suspicious looking men. He kept his hand near the small of his back where his gun was tucked.

"Y'all play it cool so they don't know we're on to them—Remember, we want the element of surprise on our side," Murtaugh said as he adjusted his shades. He had both of his hands on his hips. He was a righty so his gun was on his right side, and he was ready to go at the first sign of trouble.

A very sweaty Joaquin had his back against Mekhi's chest and was backing him down, heading toward the basket. Joaquin faked like he was going to go to his right twice and then he spun off Mekhi, taking the basketball to his left. As soon as he left Mekhi's side, the side of his dome exploded. A bullet went through one side of his temple and came out of the side of the other. His brain fragments and blood splashed upon the ground while he fell toward his left.

Joaquin was ignorant of what had just happened to his opponent. He took two long strides before leaping into the air with the basketball, tongue hanging out of his mouth, like Michael Jordan. Taking the basketball into both hands, he slam dunked it and held onto the rim. He screamed triumphantly and raised his knees up to his chest. Lost in his glory, he was ignorant of the spectators running for lives around him screaming, bellowing and hollering.

"Somebody is shooting!" a young black girl with her hair braided in individual braids hollered out. She was running across the court with her two-year-old son pressed against her and praying she didn't get hit. One of the players on Joaquin's team ran across her, tripping over Mekhi's dead body and falling to the asphalt.

Joaquin dropped down to the ground on his bending knees. As soon as he stood upright, one of the D-boys that were attending the game ran across him, holding a black gun, icy platinum chain jumping on his chest as he ran. He'd nearly cleared Joaquin's path when another shot ripped through the air. The sniper's bullet entered the D-boy's ear and blew a big ass hole in the opposite side of his head. His limp form crashed to the court. He had a dead expression on his face, eyes wide, mouth hanging open. Blood poured out of his head and quickly pooled around it.

"What the fuck!" Joaquin said, looking down at the D-boy's body shockingly. Ducking low, he scanned the area for where the shot had come from. He couldn't tell, so he looked for Murtaugh who he'd given his gun to hold while he played basketball.

Looking up across the street at the building the shot had rang from, Aztec saw the sniper with his Nighthawk rifle in the window. His head whipped around in Joaquin's direction, and he saw the dead D-boy at his feet. He then looked at Mekhi lying lifeless in the middle of the court. That's when he realized the shooter was trying to take Joaquin out. Aztec moved to take action. Charging in Joaquin's direction, he snatched his sunglasses off and slung them aside. En route to Joaquin, he switched hands with his shotgun and shouted a warning to him.

"Joaquinnnn!" Aztec called aloud and pointed to the tenement that the sniper's bullet had come from.

Chapter 7

Joaquin's head whipped around to Aztec and then around to the building he was pointing at. It was then that he acknowledged that the shooter was trying to blow him away specifically. Everything seemed to be moving in slow motion to him and Aztec at the same time. The audience was running rampantly in pandemonium from the silent death of Mekhi. They ran back and forth across the court, trying to avoid being hit, and taking cover behind anything they could.

Meanwhile, the suspicious looking niggaz in sunglasses and hoodies shoved panicking people out of their way violently, clearing a path to where Joaquin was up the court. Zipping down their hoodies, they reached inside of them and pulled out semi-automatic handguns with silencers on them. At this same time, Hugo and Murtaugh were shoving people out of their way. Their eyes were glued to the killaz rocking the sunglasses and hoodies. They knew they had to move fast, or Aztec and Joaquin were a couple of dead men.

Still holding his concealed shotgun, Aztec leaped across the air and tackled Joaquin. Together, they crashed to the asphalt and the side of Joaquin's head ricocheted off it. He winced, feeling a bloody cut instantly opening on the side of his dome. Seeing the niggaz in the hoodies about to point their guns at them, Aztec rolled over Joaquin and placed his body between him and the killaz. He brought his shotgun around and racked that bitch, pointing it at them. A few shots were fired that struck the concrete and sent debris into the air. Narrowing his eyelids into slits, Aztec clutched his shotgun with both hands and pulled its trigger. The shotgun recoiled and released a blast, blowing one of the killaz completely off his feet. The force of the impact was so strong that it knocked the sunglasses off his face and sent him hurling backward. By this time, Hugo and Murtaugh aimed and fired their guns. Their gunshots rang out into the bright sunny day, and their bullets pelted the opposition. The opposition turned and sent some shots their way, but Aztec let his shotgun continue to fire, taking out another one of them. A minute and a half later, the killaz in the hoodies were lying down on the court, and pools of blood were forming beneath them.

Gun smoking, Hugo and Murtaugh approached the killaz who they'd laid down. Aztec was on the opposite side of the court, pulling Joaquin upon his feet and helping him brush the dust off him. Joaquin said something to him in Spanish before hurriedly retreating from off the court. Aztec made sure he'd gotten where he intended to be before walking over to where his comrades were. Together, they stood over the killaz they'd flat-lined. Aztec harped up some thick nasty mucus and spat it down on the face of one of the men. The glob of mucus plummeted and splattered against the faces of one of the executed.

"Y'all, come on! The shooter is somewhere up in that complex!" Aztec ran toward the apartment building where Asad was holed up, and pointed up at it. Hugo and Murtaugh ran alongside him. Murtaugh spat the plan he had in mind to catch the son of a bitch that had tried to kill Joaquin.

***

Seeing Joaquin and his goons had discovered where he was holed up, Asad snatched his rifle out of the window and ran out of the boy's bedroom. He hung a left out of the door and ran up on the front door, unlocking it. He snatched it open and darted out of the door, running out into the hall-way. Asad looked up and down the hallway for a quick place to escape. He didn't see one, so he hurried down to three flights of stairs. Reaching the landing of the next floor, he kicked open the door and darted out into the hallway.

Asad searched the corridor for another place to make his getaway. When his eyes landed on the window at the end of the hall, he ran at it, firing his rifle and cracking its glass. Having weakened the window's glass, he threw down his rifle and dove through the glass like he was diving into a swimming pool. The broken pieces of glass went along with Asad as he hurled below, swinging his arms and kicking his legs.

"Ugh!" Asad said aloud, making a soft landing inside of the trash bin and tipping it over. He spilled out onto the graveled ground, twinkling pieces of broken glass peppering his head and shoulders. Asad scrambled to his feet and looked down at the end of the alley. Hugo and Murtaugh had just run into the end of it. Murtaugh tapped Hugo for his attention and pointed in Asad's direction. They then took off running toward that direction.

Asad looked around for somewhere to escape. Running forward, he leaped up and grasped the top of the brick wall and pulled himself over. He jumped down to the ground and landed on his bending knees, taking off running. As soon as he sprinted across the lawn of the backyard, a Rottweiler ran out of his dog house, barking, bypassing a big cream-colored dog bowl labeled *Satan*.

"Woof, woof, woof, woof, woof!" The Rottweiler barked savagely at Asad, chasing after him, snapping at his heels. Feeling the threat of the dog at his heels seemed to make Asad run faster. Glancing over his shoulder, he saw the beast snapping dangerously close at his heels.

"Oh, fuck!" Asad's eyes got big, as he hollered aloud. Seeing refuge in another yard ahead, he took three big long strides and prepared to jump. As Asad's sneakers left the grass, so did Satan's paws. The mean old hound was in midair when the chain around his spiked, black leather collar snatched him back. Satan landed back down on his paws while Asad planted his sneaker firmly against the brick wall and hoisted himself over it.

Asad had gotten halfway over the wall when he looked up. Hugo was climbing the brick wall he'd already gotten over, while Murtaugh was coming at him. Seeing him lifting his gun to take a shot at him, Asad dropped down from the brick wall and took off running.

"Shit, shit, shit!" Murtaugh angrily swung and punched the air, missing his chance to pick Asad off the brick wall. He looked at the corner of his eye and saw Satan coming at him fast, saliva dripping from his fanged mouth. "Oh, fuck!" His eyes got big, seeing the vicious beast headed his way.

Murtaugh was about to shoot him, but then he heard a gunshot from behind him. The dog yelped painfully and retreated back toward his house, bleeding. Making note of him getting away, Hugo, who'd shot him the first time, aimed his gun at him again. Clutching his gun with both hands, he squeezed his left eyelid shut and pulled its trigger. A bullet ripped through the air and zeroed in on Satan's skull, blowing his bloody brain fragments against his dog house.

"Te veo en el cielo perrito, hijo de puta! (*See you in doggy heaven, mothafucka!*)" Hugo said, looking over at the dead Rottweiler's body. Looking ahead, he saw Murtaugh sitting at the top of the brick wall with his hand extended downward. Hugo grasped a firm hold of his hand and Murtaugh helped pull him upon the wall. Together, they jumped down onto the backyard lawn of someone else's house.

***

Asad sprinted across a vacant lot filled with dirt and surrounded by gate to keep trespassers out. His sights were set on the gate ahead and the residential street beyond it. Adjusting his gun on his waistline, he ran as fast as he could toward the gate and leaped upon it. Holding on tight to it, Asad began to scale the gate. Coming over the top of it, he lost his bearings and collided with the sidewalk, grimacing. Scrambling back upon his feet, he searched the ground for his gun, which he'd dropped when he'd fallen. Once he'd located it, he picked it up and took off running. Glancing back over his shoulder, on the opposite side of the gate, Asad could see Hugo and Murtaugh chasing after him, guns in hand. Asad ran a little further down the sidewalk before slowing to a stop and turning around. Lifting his gun, he pointed it and pulled its trigger, back to back.

Choot, choot, choot, choot!

The hushed bullets ripped through the air and ricocheted off the gate, making sparks fly. Hugo and Murtaugh ducked and scrambled out of the way of gunfire, trying not to get their heads blown off. Seeing that he'd gotten them off his ass for the time being, Asad continued running up the sidewalk, huffing and puffing, still keeping a look out over his shoulder. Every now and then he'd take the time to wipe the dripping sweat from his forehead. Hearing hurried footsteps at his back, he knew Hugo and Murtaugh were on his heels again. In pursing him, they'd occasionally stop and pop shots at him.

Bloc, bloc, bloc, boc, boc, boc!

Asad ducked and zig-zagged to avoid the bullets meant to take his life. Some of them slammed into nearby parked vehicles, shattered their back windows, and ricocheted off the poles of stop signs.

"Come on! He's getting away!" Murtaugh hollered at Hugo who was having troubling keeping up. Although he was as big as a dump truck, he didn't have much stamina. He was sweaty, sticky, winded and tired. Murtaugh took two more shots at Asad before he grabbed him under his arm and hurried him along beside him. Huffing and puffing, with sweat sliding down the side of his face, Hugo wiped the side of his face with his sleeve. He then lifted his gun and licked shots at a retreating Asad.

Running, Asad's eyebrows arched and his nose scrunched up. His nostrils flared and he clenched his teeth. A vein bulged up his neck and at his temple. He felt like a straight up bitch, being chased by Hugo and Murtaugh. He hadn't been in this position before in life, and he hated it.

"Niggaz coming at me like I'ma punk and shit! I ain't no mothafucking mark! Fuck this!" Asad said to no one in particular. Slowing his running down to a job, he turned around and lifted up his gun. He pointed it and pulled the trigger again, back to back.

Choot, choot, choot, choot!

Hugo and Murtaugh ducked and scrambled out of the way of the whizzing bullets. They took cover behind a nearby parked Ford Explorer. Cautiously, Murtaugh peeked around the back of the truck and saw Asad hauling ass up the sidewalk. Hugo and Murtaugh were about to come out from behind the Ford Explorer, but Asad stopped running. Turning around, he gripped his gun with both hands and brought it up, getting off. One of the bullets cracked the windshield of the Ford Explorer while the other one knocked off its side view mirror.

Seeing he'd backed down Hugo and Murtaugh again,

Asad started back up running again. As he cut across the street, Hugo and Murtaugh emerged from behind the SUV, sending fire at him. Asad was so caught up in avoiding the danger at his back he neglected Aztec, who was charging at him. He came at him full speed ahead and swung the butt of his shotgun, which was wrapped up in his navy blue hoodie, into his chin. A ripple went through Asad's cheek and blood sprayed from his mouth. He collided with the asphalt fast and hard. His head ricocheted off the street, and his eyes rolled to their whites. Asad looked like he had Q-balls in his eye sockets as he lay on the ground, barely conscious. He moaned in pain and drooled at his mouth, warm saliva forming a small pool below him.

Panting out of breath, Hugo and Murtaugh ran upon Aztec. He'd just cocked the slide on his shotgun and pointed it down at Asad, wishing he'd make a sudden move so he could blow his brains out.

"Y'all niggaz slow as a mothafucka, man. Y'all were gon' let this nigga get away. Luckily for you, I came along!" The young nigga kicked Asad in his side hard as shit, making him howl in pain and clutch his aching side.

"Aww, shut the fuck up, Tec!" a scowling Murtaugh said to him, approaching Asad and tucking his gun at the small of his back. "Gemme that bandana you got on you." He extended his hand and wiggled his fingers, waiting for Aztec to give him his bandana. Aztec pulled the blue bandana from out of his back pocket and passed it to Murtaugh. Murtaugh used it to bind Asad's wrists behind his back. He then picked up the gun he'd dropped when Aztec had knocked him out, and tucked it at the small of his back, alongside his other gun.

"We finally got his bitch-ass," Hugo said, looking down at Asad.

"You mean, I finally got 'em," Aztec took the credit with his thumb pointed at his chest. He then lowered his shotgun at his side.

"Yeah, whatever, mothafucka, it was a team effort," Hugo insisted.

"Like he said, dick cheese, 'team effort'," Mutaugh told him, pulling a bandana from out of his back pocket and gagging Asad's mouth with it.

Presently, Aztec spoke like he was running the show. "Alright, that's enough of all that bitching! Snatch his lil' bitch-ass up and toss 'em inside the van. Make sure that gag and that bandana is secure on 'em, too. We don't want 'em getting away before we bleed 'em for all the fuck he knows."

Hugo looked up and down the street for the van Aztec was talking about. His forehead crinkled when he didn't see it. "Tec, where the fuck is the van?"

"Here it is, now." Aztec looked to his right, and a van pulled up, stopping before him. Joaquin hopped out, holding a freezer bag of ice cubes to the bleeding wound on the side of his head.

"Yo, Joaquin, are you all right?" Murtaugh asked, concerned, trying to get a good look at the side of his head.

"Yeah, I'm straight, which is more than I can say for this puta!" Joaquin kicked Asad in his mouth, instantly knocking him out cold. He lay on the concrete, snoring with a bloody grill. Hearing the police car sirens getting uncomfortably close, Joaquin looked around to see if they'd arrived on the same block they were posted up on. They hadn't. "Alright, Hugo and Murtaugh, y'all load 'em up in the van. Tec, you gon' roll with me, you're driving but leave that shotty with them."

"Fa sho'," Aztec replied and carried his shotgun over to the back of the van. He opened it and stashed it inside.

As soon as he did, Hugo and Murtaugh arrived with an unconscious Asad and dumped him inside. Afterward, they shut the back double doors of the van and moved to climb inside of it. Murtaugh told Joaquin where they were going to take Asad to torture him for information. He then fired up the van and drove off in a hurry.

"Move your ass, homeboy—Here!" Joaquin told Aztec as he tossed him his car key. Aztec caught the car key and sped walked alongside him. Ten minutes later, they were peeling away from the area.

***

A yellowing light bulb hung from the ceiling by a string with flies swarming around it. One of the flies flew away from the group and landed on top of Asad's bowed head. He was sitting unconscious and duct-taped to an iron chair. Suddenly, he was splashed with a big dirty bucket of water which woke him right up. Asad threw his head back, and his eyes bulged, behaving like he was drowning under water and someone had finally let him up to take a breath of air. He looked around, blinking his eyelids. Seeing double, he tried to focus his vision as water slid down his face and dripped off his chin, splashing on the floor.

Once Asad wasn't seeing double any more, everyone standing before him came into focus. He saw Joaquin, Hugo, Murtaugh and Aztec standing before him. Joaquin slung the big dirty bucket aside. It flew across the room and deflected off a table loaded with junk—mainly a big ass chainsaw, which had dried blood and brain fragments clinging to it. Its jagged metal blade had obviously been used to butcher several poor souls that had the misfortune of seeing it.

"Who sent chu at me? Huh? Was it that nigga God,

huh?" Joaquin looked Asad over carefully. It didn't shock him that he was so young, because he made his bones killing niggaz when he was barely old enough to piss straight. Hell, for that matter, back home in Mexico, he'd seen boys no older than eight years old put bullets into men four and five times their age. The killaz in America were just as young and seemed to have been getting younger and younger with each generation. The way Joaquin was taught: if a child was old enough to pick up a gun, then he was old enough to be killed by one. It was a mighty cold world that we lived in!

Looking around at all of the men caused Asad's heart to thud crazily, but he'd be damned if he showed these mothafuckaz he was fearful. The way he saw it, he was groomed by God, the most gangsta nigga to have ever picked up a gun, and he was going to show them how niggaz that came under him got down.

They've got me dead to rights. I already know how this is going to end. So, I may as well drop my nuts and let 'em hang on these bitch-ass niggaz! Asad thought, as he spat on the ground and looked Joaquin in the eye, menacingly.

"I'm not telling you jack shit!" Asad told him defiantly.

Joaquin scowled, feeling disrespected that Asad hadn't answered his question. He lifted his open hand up and above his shoulder. He was about to bring his hand down and across Asad's face, until he felt someone tapping his shoulder. He looked over his shoulder and found Aztec pulling black leather gloves over his hands. His face was fixed with a frown, and he was staring down Asad.

"Step aside, bro, I got this fool," Aztec assured, punching his gloved fists into each of his palms, making sure they were snuggly fitted. Asad continued to stare down at Aztec as he approached him. Joaquin, Murtaugh and Hugo stood on the sidelines, watching him attentively.

Grabbing the front of Asad's shirt with one hand, Aztec lifted the other high above his shoulder and brought it down with all his might. The back of his hand came across Asad's face so viciously it split his bottom lip and bloodied his mouth. The impact of the blow made his eyes roll back to their whites, and his head hung back lazily. A red hand impression was on the side of Asad's face, and it was stinging immensely. In fact, the entire side of his face was beginning to swell. Aztec may have been a little man, but he was undeniably strong, possessing the might of two and a half men—arguably.

Still holding the front of Asad's shirt, Aztec scowled and bit down on his bottom lip. He continued to whip his gloved hand back and forth across his face, turning his face redder and redder. Aztec released the front of Asad's shirt and took his step back, watching him closely. He blinked his eyes continuously, trying to gather his wits as slimy ropes of blood hung from his bottom lip.

"Now, who sent chu at my big bro? I suggest you give us some answers 'fore I fuck around and beat chu to death in this fucking basement!" Aztec told Asad, as he stood over him, balled fists at his sides.

Asad poked at a loose tooth inside his mouth that he'd gotten from Aztec's brutal assault. He looked up at Aztec with a grill filled with blood. "Like I told yo' punk-ass homeboy, 'I'm not telling you jack shit', you fucking wetback!" He harped up some bloody mucus and spat it in Aztec's face. Aztec's faced balled up hatefully, and he balled his fists tightly. Inside, he was on fire and thinking of one thousand ways he could kill Asad.

Asad started laughing maniacally at Aztec. Slowly, his maniacal laughter grew louder and louder. He threw his head back and laughed louder than he ever had before.

"Oh, ya veo, crees que estoy jodiendo witchu eh, perra? Bueno. Bueno. Bueno, juguemos entonces, gilipollas. (*Oh, I see, you think I'm fucking around witchu huh, bitch? Okay. Okay. Well, let's play then, asshole*)." Aztec pulled off his wife beater and balled it up, using it to wipe the blood from his face. Walking over to the table, he laid his wife beater upon it and picked up the chainsaw. Seeing him doing this, Murtaugh and Hugo exchanged glances, as they wondered what his itty bitty ass had in mind.

Holding the chainsaw firmly in his hand, Aztec gave its drawstring three strong tugs before its motor came alive, and its jagged blade buzzed loud and dreadfully. Slowly, Aztec approached Asad as he continued to laugh like he'd lost his fucking mind. He saw the chainsaw coming at him and knew he was in for a world of unbearable agony. Still, that didn't stop him from laughing. As a matter of fact, Asad was laughing harder and harder, more and more, veins pronounced on his neck and forehead.

"Bienvenido a la casa del dolor! *Welcome to The House of Pain!*" Aztec smiled wickedly and narrowed his eyelids into slits, bringing the blade of the chainsaw down on Asad's shoulder.

As soon as the sharp metal tore into Asad's flesh, blood sprayed into Aztec's face and the side of Asad's neck. Asad maniacal laughter dissolved into bloody curdling screams. His eyeballs nearly popped out of their sockets, and his mouth stretched wide open, displaying all of his teeth. He could literally feel the blade cutting through his tendon and shoulder bone. More and more blood splattered against Aztec, but he kept on cutting until Asad's severed arm smacked down on the floor. By this time, Asad's eyes rolled to their whites, and his head laid aside. He'd passed out from shock.

His being unconscious didn't stop Aztec though. His little ass was determined to finish the task at hand. He went on to cut off Asad's other arm, both of his legs and then finally his head. Once he'd finished, he was covered in blood from head to toe, looking like he'd been swimming inside a pool of it. Aztec turned off the chainsaw and dropped it at his feet, where blood dripped from its blade. He scanned the floor for Asad's severed head and smiled once he'd located it. He made his way across the floor, dripping blood and leaving bloody sneaker imprints behind in his wake.

Using both hands, Aztec picked up Asad's severed head and looked down at his face. His eyes were wide, and his mouth was stuck open. His facial expression was of a man that had died in excruciating pain.

"And for my latest piece, I'd like to call this El rostro de la muerte!" Aztec announced to no one in particular.

Murtaugh frowned up. He didn't know Spanish, so he wasn't sure of what the hell Aztec had said the name of his piece was.

"The Face of Death!" Joaquin and Hugo answered in unison. They'd seen the confused look on Murtaugh's face.

Aztec approached Joaquin with Asad's severed head, leaving a trail of blood behind him. Smiling, he stopped before Joaquin and extended Asad's head toward him. "I'd like you to have it, bro. It's my gift to you. Maybe you can hang it up in your house somewhere."

"You motherfucking Mexicans are loco!" Murtaugh told Hugo. Hugo responded with a grin, and folded his arms across his chest.

Holding Asad's severed head in one hand, Joaquin looked down at it, and then back up at Aztec. "Good looking out, pequeño hermano." He slapped hands with Aztec and gave him a one arm hug, bloodying his clothes.

Aztec walked over to the table and picked up his wife beater, wiping his face clean of Asad's blood.

Chapter 8

Ammura sat at the small table at the center of her living room floor. She was a beautiful, mahogany-toned young lady with light-brown eyes. She rocked a fade with an abstract design pattern on either side of her head, and a diamond stud nose-ring in her right nostril. Her three-year-old baby girl, Aziza, who was the spitting image of her, filled her small pink tea cup with water, pretending it was apple cinnamon tea.

"There you go, miss. That will be one dollar and fifty-five cents." Aziza told her how much her tea would cost her. She was wearing a backward cap and an apron, acting as if she really worked at a store that served tea to customers.

"Wow. You guys are expensive. You went up. It used to be a buck twenty-five for apple cinnamon tea here." Ammura pulled out an imaginary dollar and fifty-five cents, passing it to her daughter who put it inside of her toy register.

Hearing knocking at the front door, Ammura kissed Aziza on the cheek and told her she'd be right back. She made her way to the front door and looked through its peephole, seeing the FedEx delivery man. He was a five-foot-five fella wearing a cap with the company's logo pulled low over his brows and his matching uniform. Although Ammura couldn't clearly see his face, judging from his complexion, she believed he was someone of Spanish origin. Ammura went on to unchain and unlock the door before pulling it open.

"Hey, how're you doing?" the short delivery man greeted her, but didn't bother looking up into her face. Though she found this odd, she shrugged, greeted him and signed the necessary document. Right after, the delivery man unloaded the six boxes from his dolly and sat them down inside of her living room. He was about to leave, until Ammura called him back.

"Don't forget your tip." Ammura smiled and out-stretched her hand, which had a folded five-dollar bill in it.

"Thank you," the delivery man said before plucking the money from out of her hand and making his way out of the door.

"Have a nice day!" Ammura said, as he crossed the threshold onto the front porch. The delivery man didn't reply. Instead he lifted his hand, in way of a response, and went on about his business, to make his other deliveries.

"Well, that was a strange encounter," Ammura said to no one in particular, shutting and locking her door. As she was turning around, Aziza was entering the living room, eyeballing the boxes that had just been delivered.

"What in the boxes, mommy?" Aziza asked curiously.

"I don't know yet, baby—We've gotta open it and see," Ammura told her, as she returned from the kitchen with a steak knife. She sat Indian style on the floor and pulled one of the boxes into her. Aziza looked over her mother's shoulder as she slit opened the box. Holding the steak knife in one hand, she opened the box, which was filled with balls of Styrofoam. She was about to take out whatever was inside when the telephone rang. "That's probably your daddy, baby girl. Lemme go see."

Ammura ventured off to her bedroom to answer the telephone. While she was gone, a curious Aziza rifled through the box her mother had slit open, spilling Styrofoam balls everywhere.

"Girl, I thought chu was my man calling," Ammura said, as she walked past the living room, where Aziza was rummaging through the box, heading toward the bathroom. Entering, she raised the lid of the commode and slipped her panties down around her ankles. As soon as she plopped down onto the toilet seat, she began to relieve her bladder. "Oh, yeah, well, when is JoJo's party?"

Meanwhile, Aziza pulled out something oval-shaped and wrapped in plastic bubble wrap. A smile spread across her angelic face looking at it. She then ran toward the hallway, falling and dropping the item that was wrapped in the bubble wrap. Scrambling back upon her feet, she picked what she'd dropped up and ran inside the hallway.

"Mommy, mommy, mommy!" Aziza called out to her mother. She'd looked in her bedroom and her mother's bedroom, but she wasn't there. "Mommy, are you in the bathroom?"

"Hold on, girl, my baby is calling me," Ammura said to her friend who was on the telephone. "Yes, Aziza, what is it, baby?"

Aziza didn't respond, but Ammura could hear her little feet making hurried footsteps in her direction. Listening to her running made a smile spread across her face; she loved baby girl with all of her heart. Hearing Aziza fall, Ammura bowed her head and shook it. Her baby was so clumsy.

"Are you okay, baby?" Ammura asked her daughter. "Girl, she tripped and fell," Ammura whispered to her homegirl on the phone.

"I'm okay, mommy."

Ammura looked to the doorway, and her forehead furrowed. For the first time, she noticed something wrapped in plastic bubble wrap. She figured Aziza had dropped it when she fell.

"Baby girl, did you get that out of that box I'd opened? Is that a toy?" Ammura inquired, seeing Aziza picking up the oval-shaped item in the plastic bubble wrap.

"No, mommy, it's not a toy, silly," Aziza laughed and turned the bubble wrapped item around to her mother. "It's daddy."

The oval-shaped item wrapped in plastic bubble wrap was Asad's severed head. His eyes were bulging, and his mouth was wide open. His facial expression was of him screaming in unbearable agony.

"Oh, my god! Oh, Jesus!" Ammura's glassy eyes bulged, and her mouth quivered. Her entire body trembled, and she dropped the cordless telephone. "Aaaaaaah, aaaaaah, aaaaaah!" She screamed in torment over and over again. Tears coated her cheeks and dripped off her chin, splashing on the floor.

"Ammura, what's the matter? What's going on over there?" Ammura's friend shouted over the telephone, worried.

***

A devilish smile spread across Aztec's face, as he heard Ammura's tormented screams. He turned his FedEx cap backward, lit up the roach end of his blunt, blew out a cloud of smoke, and cranked up his car. Once he glanced at his side view mirror and saw there weren't any oncoming vehicles, he busted a U-turn and drove off in the opposite direction.

Mission accomplished!

***

"So, you mean to tell me that God is your daughter's mother's fiancé and the guy reigning over the territory you wanna procure? Man, it sure is a small world," Murtaugh said to Joaquin, as they stood in his basement.

"Yeah, and what the fuck you mean it's a small world? You know 'em or something?" Joaquin inquired.

"As a matter of fact, I do," Murtaugh told him, shaking a fistful of peanuts. "The God you're talking about is the same guy who contracted you to take out Frog, on the inside, remember?"

Joaquin massaged his chin, as he thought about what he'd been told. A light bulb of recognition came on inside of his head, as he recalled the hit he'd taken on Frog. He'd killed many men inside and outside the walls of jail. So, naturally, it was hard for him to remember exactly who Murtaugh was referring to.

"I know who you're talking about now," Joaquin said, nodding. "What chu know about 'em?"

"Well, for starters, I know he's one of the biggest drug dealers on his side of the city," Murtaugh told him.

Joaquin's eyebrows rose surprisingly. "Is that so?"

"Yep, and he owes it all to Ms. Jones, or Momma Jones, as she's affectionately called by the dope boys around the way." Murtaugh nodded and threw back some more peanuts.

"Wait a minute, this old bitch is a crackhead?" Joaquin asked curiously.

"Exactly. But she works exclusively for God." Murtaugh dropped that bit of knowledge on him. He then sat his milkshake aside on the table. "You see, Momma Jones is the old bitch that cooks up God's drugs. She has a mean ass recipe for whipping coke into crack. It's that recipe that has made God a Million-Dollar Man." What Murtaugh just revealed had Joaquin thinking and rubbing his hands together greedily. He knew that if he could get Ms. Jones' recipe for cooking crack, he could propel himself into another tax bracket in a matter of months. Joaquin started formulating a plan inside of his head when Hugo came walking down the staircase.

"Fuck y'all talking about?" Hugo asked as he approached.

"I just came up with a plan that's going to make us all millionaires," Joaquin told him excitedly.

"Well, shit, that's one plan I don't mind hearing," Hugo said and folded his arms across his chest.

"Me too." Murtaugh smiled and patted Hugo on his shoulder.

"I'ma bring y'all up to speed, but I think it's best if I get Tec over here first so I won't have to repeat this shit again," Joaquin said, as he pulled out his cell phone and hit up Aztec. The young man was there in thirty minutes flat. He dapped up Murtaugh and Hugo, and Joaquin informed them of his plan. They all agreed to come onboard with Joaquin's plan and the parts they'd play in it.

"Murtaugh and Hugo, I'ma need y'all to start making those moves tonight," Joaquin told them. "As far as you, Tec, I need you to execute every man on this list." He passed him a sheet of spiral notebook paper with a list of drug dealers' names on it. Right below the names were addresses where these men could possibly be found.

Joaquin understood that if he was going to take over Watts, he was going to have to play chess—not checkers. He couldn't just go to niggaz hoods and open up shop. Nah, he had to eliminate the key players in the game before he moved in on their territories. "Once you've gotten these fools outta the way, we'll bring their workers into our operation and have 'em working for us."

Aztec looked up from the list of names and said, "What if these fools aren't trying to get with our program?"

Joaquin was silent for a moment before finally answering. "Easy. You do what you do best."

Aztec smiled devilishly. He loved putting in work, so he was hoping the opposition wasn't trying to fuck with them just so he could kill some shit. "I got chu faded, dog." He dapped up Joaquin.

"As far as any other hustlers out there getting money, you tell 'em from now on they buy from me—if they're not trying to do that then show 'em your talents," Joaquin told him, referencing to him to kill the street niggaz who weren't trying to buy their product from him.

Aztec stared at the information on the sheet of paper a little while longer until he memorized it. Whipping out a Zippo lighter, he produced a flame and held it at the end of the sheet of paper. The paper turned black and curled up, fire devouring it. Seeing Joaquin looking at him like something was wrong with him, Aztec decided to explain himself.

"I've got all of this up here, bro," Aztec assured him, as he tapped his finger against his temple. "Wouldn't want the policia getting a hold of this. This bit of info is enough to send your boy to the pen."

Joaquin nodded understandingly.

"Alright, we're finna get up outta here, man—We've got work to do," Murtaugh said, dapping up Joaquin and Aztec. Hugo was right behind him, doing the same. He and Murtaugh then made their way up the staircase.

Once they'd left, Joaquin moved the dryer back from the wall and grabbed a black gun case. He laid the gun case down on the dryer and popped its locks, lifting its lid. He then turned the gun case around so it would be facing Aztec. Inside of the case, there was a ghost gun (an untraceable gun) with a silencer attachment, box of ammunition and extra magazines.

Aztec picked up the ghost gun, loading it and cocking its slide. He aimed it at different shit inside of the basement, imagining himself blowing out the brains of the men listed on the sheet of paper.

"You feeling that?" Joaquin asked Aztec with a grin, watching him toy with the ghost gun.

"Yeah, I fucks with this, bro." Aztec smiled as he examined the gun.

Joaquin's cell phone rang and he answered it. He disconnected the call shortly after and told Aztec to answer the door.

"Alright, I'll be right back," Aztec said, as he sat the silenced handgun down in its gun case and headed up the staircase.

Aztec returned shortly with two men following behind him. They were wearing black motorcycle helmets and were clad in black leather motorcycle suits. They also had katanas sheathed on their backs. As they advanced in Joaquin's direction, they pulled off their helmets and tucked them under their arms. The first one was a light-skinned kid with a face covered in freckles. He had naturally curly hair which he wore in box braids. The other, standing at six-foot-one, which was an inch taller than his partner, was a brown-skinned dude. He rocked a small tapered afro and goatee. These men were menacing in appearance and wore the title of 'killaz' proudly.

"Allow me to make the introductions," Joaquin said, clearing his throat. He then extended his hand toward the two leather clad motorcyclists, "Tec, meet Marquette and La'Quan. Maquette and La'Quan, meet my lil' bro Tec."

These motorcyclists were the men hired to knock off the main competitors in the territories Joaquin wished to sell his product.

"What's up?" Aztec touched fists with Marquette first. He was the light-skinned one. He then touched fists with La'Quan, who was the taller brown-skinned one. Marquette and La'Quan didn't say much upon greeting. Although they were men of few words, they were prone to get violent. This was the reason why Joaquin had put them on his payroll.

"Alright, bro, I'ma go ahead and bust these moves with these boys," Aztec told Joaquin, as he shut and locked the gun case. He picked it up by its handle and dapped up Joaquin, touching his fist to his chest. Afterward, he walked toward Marquette and La'Quan.

"Y'all niggaz take care of my lil' bro," Joaquin called out to them as they headed up the staircase.

***

"Alright, I'ma come by there in like an hour," God told the caller once he glanced at his digital timepiece. "Peace." He disconnected the call and held his cell phone at his side. He took a deep breath and slipped his cell phone inside of his pocket. When he turned around, he found Billie standing behind him with a concerned look on her face. She'd picked up from the expression on his face that something was noticeably troubling him.

"Who was that?" Billie questioned him as she journeyed further inside of their bedroom. She stood before God and folded her arms across her bosom, switching her weight to her other foot.

"Asad's baby's mama—he's dead," a teary eyed God regretfully informed her. She could see the hurt threatening to spill down his cheeks, and she didn't want to do anything more than comfort him.

"Oh, baby, I'm so sorry. Come here." Billie pulled him

close and wrapped her arms around him; he peered over her shoulder, with tears threatening to spill out of his eyes. He loved Asad like he was his sibling. The young nigga was as good as blood to him, as far as he was concerned. And the mothafucka responsible for his death would pay dearly.

"Do they know who did it?" Billie asked, as she broke their embrace and held him at arm's length, staring into his eyes.

God nodded and said, "I know exactly who got at the little homie." His fists balled up at his sides.

Billie angled her head and looked at him, like, *I know it's not Joaquin.* God nodded by way of an answer, and she looked away. She knew right then that he had revenge on his mind, and she doubted if she could change his mind.

"I already know what you're thinking, and you should just go ahead and make peace with it 'cause it's gonna happen," God said.

Billie became angry, and she whipped around to him. "Wait a minute—I know you don't think I'm going to be cool with you killing the father of my child."

"Nope. But are you gonna be cool with the father of your child killing your husband?" He approached her, placing his strong vein-riddled hands on her stomach that was beginning to protrude. He looked her directly in her eyes. "Have you forgotten that I am also the father of our unborn child?"

"No, I haven't forgotten. How could I?"

"I don't know, you tell me. 'Cause on some real shit, you acting like his life is the only one that matters right now. Besides you, Annabelle, and our unborn, I also have Charity to worry about. And I for damn sure don't want lil' mama growing up without a father like I did."

"So, what are you tryna say?" Billie asked him as her

eyes filled with tears which spilled down her cheeks.

Cupping her face in his hands, God looked her in her eyes and said, "Stop crying, baby. You know what those tears do to a nigga's heart." He wiped her tears away with his thumbs. "I'ma keep it a stack witchu, ma. Even if I wanted to turn back now, I couldn't. Far too much has happened between yo' baby daddy and me. Not only that, but I made a blood oath to Asad before he died."

"A blood oath?" Billie asked, frowning. She'd never heard of a blood oath before.

"Yeah, a blood oath," God said as he approached his dresser's mirror. He plucked the photo from the corner of the mirror and looked at it. He, Country, Buck Wild and Asad was in it. They'd taken the photo one night at the club. They were in their best drip, flashing money, jewelry, and expensive gold bottles of champagne. He remembered that event vividly. They'd all gone out to celebrate Asad's birthday. They'd had a ball! "A blood oath is an oath taken by two or more people in which they ceremonially use or exchange each other's blood. To break a blood oath is punishable by death. The spiritual realm will see to it that you pay that debt—Me, Country and Buck Wild made a blood oath to Asad..."

***

God, Country and Buck Wild were down inside of his basement. They were all dressed in black leather aprons and black gloves. They carried around a box of white rodents each, feeding the exotic animals that God kept housed there. God had a total of one hundred reptiles that he housed down inside of his basement. He absolutely loved his animals. Sometimes he found himself chilling down in the basement within, twisted up a fat ass blunt and chopping it up with them. Now, some of the animals God housed were illegal in the United States but he didn't give a fuck. The way he saw it, the government did illegal shit; so why couldn't he?

Busters do what they can, bosses do what they want, God thought as he dropped a white red eyed rat inside of his pet python's cage and quickly closed it shut. He focused his eyes on the aquarium as the rat moved dangerously close to the python. Within the blink of an eye, the python lunged forward, sunk its fangs into the rodent, and rapidly wrapped its eight-foot-long greenish black body around it. The snake went right to work, squeezing the life out of the rat. God was thoroughly entertained as he watched the life flicker out inside of the furry white creature's eyes. It arms and legs flailed swiftly on and off until he eventually stopped moving altogether.

God, with a blunt hanging from his mouth, focused his attention on a colorful glossy flyer. The flyer was a promotional invite to a basketball game going down in the hood. Playing in the game was the exact man that God was looking to take off his feet, Joaquin. A fine-ass redbone with afro puffs had given the promotional flyer to Asad while he was pumping gas into his car. Asad was surprised when he saw Joaquin's face on the flyer and couldn't wait to get the news to God.

Asad knew the area where the basketball game was taking place like the back of his hand. On the drive over to God's house, he devised a plan to get close enough to Joaquin to take his head off. And if he should miss, he had a backup plan that would be on the ground level to make sure his black ass wouldn't see another day.

God nodded approvingly when Asad told him his plan. It was well-orchestrated, and he had a good feeling that it would actually work as well. He had planned on giving the assignment to another one of his angels, but Asad insisted on it being him that carried out the mission. Since it was Asad that had brought him the information and came up with the plan, God felt like it was only right that he was assigned the task.

"Country," God called out to his homeboy. As soon as he turned around, he tossed him the key to a door he was standing beside. Country was in the middle of feeding some baby crocodiles some mice. "Open that closet door and grab that long black gun case outta there for me, big dog. Please. I appreciate it."

"No problem," Country told him, as he sat the brown paper box of mice down. He then opened the closet door and grabbed the black gun case by its handle. Once he locked the closet door back, he carried the gun case over to God and handed it to him.

God popped the locks on the long case and revealed a MPA 338BA Bolt Action Rifle, with a suppressor on it. He stuck his blunt into his mouth, picked the rifle up, made sure it wasn't loaded and passed it to Asad. A serious look was plastered across Asad's face as he took the MPA 338BA Bolt Action Rifle from God. He hoisted the Bolt Action Rifle up, bracing it against his shoulder, and looking through its lens. He aimed the rifle at different animals' aquariums before placing it back inside of its case and locking it.

"You sure you can handle this mission?" God asked him, as he took the blunt from out of his mouth and blew out a big ass cloud of smoke.

"My nigga, you already know how I'm onnit," Asad assured him. He was well aware that God knew about how he'd given it up in the streets.

"Good," God said, patting him on his shoulder.

Asad became quiet as he massaged his chin, thinking on the assignment he was taking on. God's forehead wrinkled, wondering what was on his mind.

"What's the deal, young nigga?" God inquired.

"Just thinking, man, this is a very serious mission I'm taking on. A nigga may or may not make it out alive. Should that happen, I'd like to know that y'all got the niggaz that got me—and that my fiancée and my baby girl is well taken care of."

"Bruh, we all like family so you know we gon' flat-line any busters that stop you from making it back to yo' fam," Buck Wild told him.

"Yeah, shawty, and you know niggaz gon' take care of yo' fiancée and yo' lil' girl," Country assured him.

"I put my stamp on what the homies are saying," God chimed in, placing his hand on Asad's shoulder. "Should anything happen to you, niggaz gon' feel our pain and yo' family is gonna be taken care of. You've got my word, yo' lady and yo' lil' mama is notta gonna want for anything."

"Y'all niggaz willing to take a blood oath?" Asad looked around at all of their faces. God, Buck Wild and Country exchanged glances and shrugged.

"Aye, lil' bro, if its gon' make you feel secure when you go to give this fuck-nigga Joaquin his issue, then we're down with taking that oath," God told him.

"Okay." Asad nodded and pulled out his hunting knife where he had it sheathed at the small of his back. The curved tip of it twinkled and he jabbed himself in the palm, wincing.

Once blood oozed out of the small puncture wound in Asad's palm and formed a bubble, he passed the knife to Buck Wild. Buck Wild pulled off one of his black gloves and jabbed the palm of his hand, drawing blood. God and Country went on to do the same to themselves before passing the knife back to Asad.

"Alright, I suppose Country and I will go first," Asad extended his hand to Country as it dripped blood, splashing on the floor and the tip of his sneaker. Country, palm dripping blood, grasped Asad's hand. They held one another's gaze. "Repeat after me: I solemnly swear that if my blood brother should perish on his mission that I, Big Country, along with the rest of my brothers, will enact revenge on his behalf. As his blood brother, I also promise to make sure that his family is financially, spiritually, physically and emotionally taken care of. If I should ever break this blood oath, may I meet a tragic death and my soul burn in hell for all eternity."

Once Asad and Country finished reciting the words together, they gave each other a brotherly hug and patted each other's back. Asad then carried out the same ritual with Buck Wild and God.

***

God placed the photo back where he'd taken it. He pulled open the top drawer of his dresser and reached under his folded clothing. He pulled Asad's gold rope chain with the lion's head medallion from the drawer, and looped it around his neck. Asad had given it to him to hold until he came back from assassinating Joaquin. God stared at it, seething with anger and balling his fists. He made up his mind then that he'd wear the chain for the rest of his life in remembrance of his fallen brother, Asad Muhammad.

"Wait a minute, you mean to tell me that Asad got at Joaquin?" Billie asked him.

"Yeah, but the young nigga missed." God shook his head regretfully. "Something told me not to let that boy carry out that hit, but I didn't listen. Damn, Asad! Damn!" He slammed his fist into his palm heatedly.

"Baby, I'm sorry about your friend, but you've gotta understand my position," Billie said. "Now, Joaquin may be your enemy but he still is Annabelle's father. You keep that in mind when you go to take him out 'cause it's gonna hurt her when she finds out about his death. And what hurts her hurts me as well. I know I can't deter you from seeking out revenge 'cause you're just as stubborn as Joaquin is. So, I'll only ask that when you do handle him—make sure he's able to have an open-casket funeral—for Annabelle's sake."

God lowered his head and thought about what Billie said, running his hand down his face. He lifted his head back up and said, "Okay—I can do that—I can do that for lil' mama."

"Thank you," Billie said, managing a smile. She was surprised with her request. Although she didn't want to see either God or Joaquin murdered, she knew she had to be completely loyal to the man she loved. He was her husband, so it was him who she wanted to come home to once all of this was over.

"You're welcome, baby," God replied, as he cupped Billie's face and kissed her. He then got down on his knees and lifted up her gown, revealing her robust stomach. He kissed it tenderly. Then he continued to kiss it while Billie stared down at him. She had a half smile on her face, as she held the back of head, watching him kiss her stomach several times and then rub his cheek up against it, with his eyelids closed. There was an appeased expression written across his face.

"Lemme get ready before I'm here all night kissing, hugging and rubbing on you," God told her as he stood upright.

"Hey, I wouldn't complain." Billie smiled at him, throwing her arms around his neck and staring deeply into his eyes while he held her by her waist.

"Ummmm huh, I bet chu wouldn't. Now, gemme some of them lips." God leaned forward and kissed her romantically, slipping her just a little bit of tongue. "I better get going to see this girl. I know I'ma be over there for a couple of hours, considering the circumstances. Baby, you mind grabbing my White Sox cap and my black leather jacket for me? Oh, yeah, and putta 'bout sixty racks inside of that knapsack hanging up on the back of the closet door."

"Sure thing, babe." Billie walked off to carry out her man's request.

God buckled the GPS digital timepiece around his wrist. He then removed his blower from out of his top dresser drawer, checked its magazine, and smacked it back into the bottom of it. Cocking it, he tucked it into the small of his back and grabbed three magazines, which he slid into his pocket. When he turned around, he found Billie approaching him with his black leather jacket, the knapsack, and a black White Sox baseball cap cocked to the side on her head. God smirked at the way she looked rocking his baseball cap. She looked so cute to him. Without saying a word, God turned his back to her and allowed her to slip his leather jacket on him. Once he turned back around, Billie removed the White Sox baseball cap from her head and placed it on top of his, adjusting it to her liking. She handed God the knapsack, and he slipped one of its straps over his right shoulder. Once he'd done this, Billie cupped his face with her hands and stared into his eyes.

"I love you," Billie told him sincerely.

"Not as much as I love you," God told her before kissing her again.

God told Billie goodbye and walked out of the bedroom, making his way down the hallway. He was oblivious to the fact that Annabelle was standing on the side of the door, watching him. A sad look was fixed on her face as she watched his back. He didn't know it, but she'd heard what he'd said about murdering her father, and she didn't like it. With that information stored inside of her mind, Annabelle snuck back inside of her and Charity's bedroom, climbing back into her bed. She snuggled under the covers and stared up at the ceiling. Her eyes welled up with tears, and they spilled down the sides of her face. She cried herself to sleep that night, hating the fact that her step father wanted to have her father killed.

Chapter 9

The night was crisp and cold with the occasional gust of wind blowing debris and loose trash around. Here and there, you would see dark figures moving in the shadows, coming and going as they pleased. A Cadillac Escalade truck was parked beneath the shade of a tree. The driver, Poppa, murdered the engine of the hulking vehicle and looked at his reflection in the rearview mirror. Poppa was a five-foot-eleven, three-hundred-pound man of a golden-brown hue. He had thick eyebrows, a platinum loop nose-ring in his right nostril, and a goatee. He was wearing a red Cardinals baseball cap and a red leather jacket. He wore a platinum and diamond-studded necklace with an icy platinum tarantula, covered in black diamonds, hanging at the end of it. A matching icy platinum tarantula ring adorned his right ring finger. This was also covered in black diamonds. Poppa looked like a rapper who'd just walked off the set from filming the music video to his latest single.

Poppa glanced at the side view mirror to see if he saw the person he was looking for. When he didn't, he proceeded to pull out his cellular phone from the recess of his leather jacket. He searched his contacts until he found the number he'd programmed under 'Baby Mama', and pressed the green telephone button. As soon as he heard the ringing, he brought his cell phone to his ear, and waited for his son's mother to answer.

"Hello? Man, turn that shit down, I can't even fucking hear you?" Poppa spat annoyingly into his cellular.

Poppa once was in love with his baby mama—La'Keisha—until he found out she was fucking his best friend while she was pregnant. This brought up concerns of whether his son Micah was really his. He'd snuck and gotten a DNA test kit from CVS and swabbed his baby boy's mouth. Now he was waiting for the results to come in the mail. He made up his mind that if Micah wasn't of his lineage, he was putting La'Keisha's dog-ass to sleep, right alongside his trifling ass homeboy, Darnell. But if the child was of his flesh and blood then he'd let her be. This was the only way he'd allow her to live. Otherwise the bitch was getting exactly what her *real* baby daddy had gotten.

Poppa had dropped a few bands to a couple of Armenian gangstas to take care of Darnell. They'd gagged him, chained his wrists behind his back, and fitted him with cement shoes before dumping him into the bottom of the ocean, where he'd never be seen again.

"Hold on a sec," La'Keisha said to him. A second later, the volume of the music was turned down. "Now, what were you saying?"

"Bitch, I said. Where. In. The. Fuck. Are. You?" Poppa asked heatedly.

"Nigga, who the fuck you calling a bitch?" La'Keisha retorted, enraged.

"I'm talking to you, bitch! Now, where the fuck are you? Got me out here in this shady-ass part of town!"

"You know what? I'm not even finna go there witchu tonight, Poppa. I'm having a good day and I plan on having a damn good night too."

"Whatever, bitch, where yo punk-ass at?"

"I'll be there when I get there, you fat fucka!"

"Suck my—" Poppa cut himself short when he heard her hang up on him. He looked at his cellular like it had transformed into a rattle snake in his hands. "I swear 'fore God Almighty, I hate this ho witta passion, dog! I shoulda never put myself inna position to have a baby with this bitch!" He disconnected the call and stashed his cell phone back inside of his leather jacket.

Poppa opened the glove box and removed his all-black 10mm Remington R1 Hunter, cocking the slide on it. He slid his pistol into the waistline of his jeans and fished the roach end of his blunt out of the ashtray. Usually he'd blow one in his truck, but he'd have his son this night and he didn't want the overwhelming smell of kush lingering inside his vehicle. Poppa grabbed his lighter and sparked up the roach end of his blunt. Next, he threw open the driver's door and stepped out of the SUV, the rubber bottoms of his Timberland boots greeting the ground, one at a time. Slamming the door shut behind him, Poppa took tokes of his dwindling blunt as he gave the block a close inspection. He narrowed his eyelids, as the smoke billowed from his nostrils, its repugnant fume irritating his eyes.

Besides the occasional passerby, the neighborhood looked like a ghost town. Poppa didn't mind, though. He didn't want any witnesses around when he smacked the shit out of La'Keisha's smart mouth ass for disrespecting him. Poppa had done six years on a level-four prison yard with some of the most dangerous men America had the misfortune of birthing. So he'd be damned if he'd let some trifling skeezer from the projects come at him sideways.

"Yeah, we gon' see if this punk-bitch stands tall on that shit she said," Poppa thought aloud, as he smoked the roach end of his blunt.

He posted up beside a raggedy telephone booth, most likely the only functional one left on this side of town, and finished with the consumption of his roach. Once it was nearly touching his already blackening finger tips, he blew out smoke and dropped it to the sidewalk. He mashed it out under the heel of his Timb. He then pulled the sleeve of his leather jacket back and glanced at his platinum and diamond

AP Rolex. The time was 8:20 P.M., twenty minutes after the time he was supposed to link up with La'Keisha to pick up his son.

Poppa rested his arm on the top of the telephone booth and drummed his fingers upon it, in a rhythm. His head was on a swivel as he whistled and took in his surroundings. He looked to his left after hearing a pair of feet ambling in his direction. His eyes came across a drunken Mexican man, holding what he believed was a big bottle of liquor in a wrinkled brown paper bag. The Mexican man was dressed in a beanie, trench coat and a burgundy sweatshirt which was torn around the collar. His long stringy white hair was nearly as long as his beard. Holding the alcohol beverage in one hand, he moved up the sidewalk like he didn't have ligaments to hold his joints together.

Poppa could have sworn the Mexican man had appeared out of nowhere because he sure as hell wasn't there a minute ago. Once the drunk had gotten within spitting distance of Poppa, he caught a good whiff of his foul body odor, and his face balled up with disgust. He turned his head and pulled his shirt over his nose to avoid inhaling any more of the Mexican man's putrid smell. The Mexican man's stench was a combination of cheap liquor, sweaty butthole, and funky armpits. All was enough to make Poppa want to vomit, but somehow he managed to keep his dinner down.

The Mexican man had gotten within six feet of Poppa, when he'd stopped to take a drink of his bottle of liquor. He brought the bottle down from his lips and wiped his mouth with the back of his hand. Shutting one eyelid, the old drunk peered inside of the bottle and saw he only had a corner left.

"Guess it's time I get myself another bottle." The Mexican man finished what was left in his bottle, belched and threw it aside. The bottle exploded against the side of the curb. He straightened up and strolled down the sidewalk, revealing that he wasn't really drunk at all. He brought the sleeve of his trench coat to his lips and spoke into it. "It's him! Move in!"

Aztec, who was actually the drunken Mexican man, disappeared into the shadows of the night almost magically. Overhearing Aztec, Poppa frowned up, wondering what the fuck was going on. Instantly, two black Ducatis pulled up on him from either side. He drew his black gun and held it at his side. His head moved from left to right. The motorcyclists, still wearing their helmets, placed the kickstands on their bikes and dismounted them. They then walked in Poppa's direction.

The motorcyclist at his right, La'Quan, held up his black leather gloved hands, letting him know he wasn't there to bring him any harm. He flipped open the visor of his helmet so that he could see his eyes, and so did his partner— Marquette.

"No need to be hostile, we've come in peace," La'Quan assured him. "My employer sent me a business proposal."

"Who the fuck is your employer?" Poppa asked.

"I assure you, Mr. Dupri, you'll be informed of everything on a need-to-know basis."

"What is this business proposal you're referring to?" Poppa inquired. La'Quan proceeded to unzip his leather motorcycle suit, and Poppa pointed his gun at his face. Instantly, La'Quan held his hands up in the air again. Poppa glanced over his shoulder at Marquette who was standing perfectly still. It was as if he was a statue.

"Easy now," La'Quan told him. "I was just pulling out the card I was told to give you. It has the business proposal on it I was telling you about."

"Nigga, please," Poppa began, "I don't fucking know

you. I let chu reach inside of that tight ass suit and you're liable to pull a strap out on me. You don't survive this long in the game I'm playing in by being a goddamn fool. Whatever you've got in there, I'll get it."

Poppa pulled the card out of La'Quan's leather motorcycle suit and looked at it. Written on the card was the price per kilo Joaquin was offering, along with the taxes he was obligated to pay if he accepted the offer.

"The price is right, but as far as those taxes, notta fucking chance!" Poppa flicked the card at him and it deflected off La'Quan's helmet. "I'ma boss, nigga! Fuck I look like paying a nigga taxes to hustle on the same turf I grew up on? Homie you work for got me fucked up. So, I suggest you and yo' lil' friend breeze before I—"

Poppa's threat was cut short, as Marquette slipped under his outstretched arm and drew the katana sheathed on his back. He swung his katana so fast that it whistled through the air. Poppa tried to pull the trigger of his gun, but his finger didn't work. He looked at the hand that held his gun and it slowly slid off the rest of his arm, falling to the sidewalk. Poppa's eyes were as big as saucers, and his mouth was wide open. He couldn't believe his hand had just been severed. He tried to scream, but sound wouldn't come from his mouth.

La'Quan smiled wickedly from within his helmet, watching his partner work. He moved so swiftly with his katana that his movements were like blurs.

Snikt, snikt, snikt, snikt, snikt!

The blade of the katana whistled as it sliced through the air and went across Poppa's body. Up, down, across, up, and then down again. Once Marquette had finished slicing Poppa every way he could think of, he slid his legs apart and dipped low to the sidewalk. He sheathed his katana and stood upright, looking a horrified Poppa in his dumbfounded eyes.

Marquette's skillful attack made Poppa's wet intestines spill out and smack against the sidewalk at his feet. Half of his left arm detached and fell to the pavement beside his insides. Two lengthy blood cuts opened up on his chest, and finally, a bloody ring formed completely around his neck. As soon as Poppa's eyes rolled to their whites, Marquette kicked him hard in the chest. The impact launched his severed head forward and sent his limp body falling backward. Poppa's severed head tumbled toward La'Quan. Looking down at it, he kicked it high into the air and across the street. It bounced off the rooftop of a parked car and set off its alarm.

"Come on; let's get the fuck outta here!" La'Quan told Marquette, as he revved up his motorcycle.

Marquette waited, kicked up his kickstand and motioned someone over from the alley. Aztec ran out and climbed onto the back of the Ducati, hugging Marquette around the waist. La'Quan busted a U-turn in the middle of the street and ripped up the block in the opposite direction. Marquette performed the same action and ripped up the block right behind La'Quan.

La'Quan had dropped a couple of bands on La'Keisha to disclose the whereabouts of her baby daddy Poppa. She also provided him a list of his workers. Afterwards, they were going to see several other hustlers who were factors in the game. If they didn't want to come on board with Joaquin's regiment, then they were going to get what Poppa got, or worse.

***

Dennis, wearing a button-down and bow tie underneath an apron, moved down the grocery store aisle, mopping the floor. It had been eleven years since he'd gotten busted for murder. He'd tried to rob an old lady for money to support his habit. It was supposed to be an easy lick on account of his victim being seventy-five-years-old, but he didn't count on the old bird putting up a fight. Dennis drew a knife, in hopes his threatening her would make her release her purse. He was wrong! The old lady lunged forward, and they fought for control of the knife. Her resistance proved she was stronger than she looked, but not nearly as strong enough for a fully grown man. Dennis and the old lady struggling for possession of the knife eventually resulted in her lying hanging halfway off the curb. The hilt of the knife was standing up in her chest. Her eyes were wide, and her mouth was hanging open. She was dead!

During his bid, Dennis promised himself he was going to give up crack. Although he did, he winded up replacing one habit with another—cigarettes! Now that he was a free man, he realized what came with his freedom—food, shelter, and bills. He needed to support himself, so he was going to need a gig. Dennis went on a job hunt, but unfortunately he had every door slammed in his face. He wanted to say, *fuck it,* and go back to running the streets smoking crack, but his determination propelled him forward.

Since Dennis couldn't find any decent jobs, he decided to start at the bottom of the totem pole, filling out applications at every fast food restaurant and supermarket he could. None of them wanted to give him a shot on account of him having a felony on his record. Desperate for money, he was going to try his hand at slinging weed, but fortune smiled on him through Mr. Jefferies. Old man Jefferies offered him a job at the supermarket around the corner from his mother's house. Dennis humbly accepted the offer. Now, the pay was shit and he kept long hours, but the gig gave him something to do, and kept his parole officer off his back.

"Dennis."

He looked up and found Mr. Jefferies standing before him. He was a tall man with a shaved head of white stubble. He rocked a black bow tie, sky blue button-down shirt and slacks. Although he was sixty-five years old, Mr. Jefferies didn't look a day over forty. He was a well-mannered, pleasant, generous man that was always willing to help others.

"When you're done here, go ahead and dump the garbage and take your break."

"Yes, sir, Mr. Jefferies," Dennis replied and continued mopping the floor.

"Boy, I done told you about calling me Mr. Jefferies, you gon' make me knock your young ass out. I done told you now!" Mr. Jefferies smiled and danced around Dennis, throwing phantom punches and jabs at him.

Dennis laughed and said, "Okay, okay, okay, Harold."

"Now, that's more like it." Mr. Jefferies grinned and patted him on his shoulder. He then headed toward the back of the store to tend to some other business.

***

Fifteen minutes later

Dennis slung the twin black garbage bags into the trash bin out back. He peeled off his latex gloves, rolled them up into each other, and tossed them in as well. Turning around, he stuck a cigarette between his lips and fished around inside of his pocket for a lighter. Once he discovered the Bic, he fired up the square and blew out smoke. His eyelids narrowed, not from the thick fog of smoke he rolled off his tongue, but from the black van that pulled up across the entrance of the alley. Murtaugh and Hugo hopped out and stepped lively in his direction. Dennis paid close attention to them as they approached.

"Fuck these two niggaz headed?" Dennis's forehead crinkled wonderingly. He started thinking about all of the dopemen and corner hustlers he'd robbed and stolen crack from when he'd been out in the streets. It dawned on him that the men approaching him could be looking for some get-back on account of his past transgressions. With that in mind, Dennis discretely pulled out a straight-razor from his back pocket. Using his thumb, he opened the razor and held it down at his side. He carried on smoking his cigarette like he hadn't noticed the two men coming toward him. As soon as he got one of them close enough to him, Dennis would launch his attack.

At the corner of his eye, Dennis saw both men draw something from where they had it hidden. One of those 'something's' looked like a gun, while the other looked like a retractable baton. His suspicions about the retractable baton was confirmed, when he saw it extend in length. Dennis realized he was in a real dangerous situation; and chances are, he wouldn't make it out alive. Still, he wasn't going to let these niggaz take him without a fight. If they wanted his life, then they'd have one hell of a time getting it.

Once Dennis noticed Hugo, the one holding the retracta-ble baton, was in striking distance, he dropped the cigarette from his lips and sprang into action. Swiftly, he swung around, bringing his straight-razor across Hugo's cheek, making him holler in agony. Hugo staggered aside, and Dennis brought the razor around again, slashing him across the side of his head. Dots of blood clung to Dennis's face and shirt.

Seeing Murtaugh lift and point his gun at him, Dennis's

eyes bulged. His heart thudded, wondering when the bullet was going to erupt from his barrel and end his life. Too bad for him, Hugo saw this as an opening for an attack and took total advantage of it. Moving extremely fast, Hugo knocked the razor out of Dennis's hand, struck him in the throat, the back of the neck, and swept his leg out from under him with his retractable baton. Dennis went up into the air and came down hard on the pavement, grimacing.

Hugo touched his cheek and the side of his head. He looked to his fingertips; they were bloody. The sight of his own blood seemed to enrage him. His face twisted in hatred and he gritted, stomping Dennis in his stomach as hard as he could. The assault made Dennis howl in pain and clutch his midsection.

"Punk mothafucka!" Hugo bellowed, touching his bleeding cheek again and looking at his fingertips. Angry again, he kicked Dennis in his side and made him bawl.

"Damn, he got chu pretty good," Murtaugh frowned as he examined Hugo's wounds. "Don't fret. We won't have to take you to a hospital. I can stitch that up myself, but it's definitely going to leave scars behind."

While Hugo was busy studying his wounds, Murtaugh approached Dennis who was pleading for his life to be spared. Little did he know, Murtaugh and Hugo weren't there to claim his life, they wanted him—alive.

"No, no, no, please!" Dennis begged while holding up his hands, palms showing. Murtaugh leveled his gun and pulled the trigger, firing a tranquilizer dart, which stuck to Dennis's chest, like a magnet. Almost instantly, Dennis's eyes became hooded and his arms dropped to his sides. He'd been put asleep.

Murtaugh tucked the tranquilizer gun into the small of his back and pulled the black pillowcase from his back pocket. He took a zip-tie from out of his pocket and pushed Dennis over onto his stomach. He bound his wrists behind his back and slipped the pillowcase over his head. As he stood upright, the black van came to a stop beside him and its driver's door opened. Hugo jumped out and made his way around to the rear of the van, opening its double doors. Together, he and Murtaugh hoisted Dennis up and placed him inside of the van. Murtaugh stood aside as Hugo slammed the double doors shut.

"Come on, let's get some glue to hold those wounds closed until I have the time to stitch 'em up," Murtaugh told Hugo and patted him on his shoulder, walking to the van to hop into the front passenger seat.

***

The basement was full of D-boys who had their eyes focused on King Midas, who'd been giving them drugs for years to push in the ghetto. King Midas was a forty-five-year-old man with skin as dark as a quarter past midnight. He had thin gold locs that spilled down his back, and a matching thick nappy beard. King Midas wore cream-colored silk shirt and slacks. There were five gold chains hanging around his neck. The gold watches and bracelets he wore on either arm nearly reached his forearm. On top of that, he wore several funny-looking gold rings on his fingers. His gold hair, teeth, jewelry and clothing all contributed to him being called King Midas.

Bloody and swollen, King Midas hung from a beam in the ceiling by a rope so tight it cut off the circulation to his hands, making them turn a bluish purple. King Midas's left eye was swollen shut, his nose was twice its size from being broken, and the entire right side of his head was the size of a basketball. In fact, that size of his dome was so monstrously large, it made him look deformed. King Midas's mouth was filled with blood, and slimy strings of it hung from his chin.

King Midas had permanent gold teeth that Aztec had took the liberty to pull out of his mouth, one by one, until he'd told him where he kept his stash of drugs and money. To King Midas's credit, he held it down for as long as he could, but unfortunately for him, he had four teeth left in total by the time La'Quan had gotten done with him.

Aztec looked at the transparent plastic bag that had King Midas's bloody gold teeth inside of it. He turned around to King Midas and held the bag up for him to see it, shaking it up and down.

"It didn't have to be this way, but this is the way you made it, homeboy," La'Quan told him. "You coulda kept yo' life and still made a living to take care of you and your family under Joaquin. But chu just hadda be greedy and keep the whole pie to yourself, huh, nigga?" La'Quan held up his finger and shook it, and then shook his head. He tossed the plastic bag of his loose bloody gold teeth aside on the floor.

"I've got it," Aztec said, as he returned to the basement with a two pillowcases full. One was loaded with money and the other was loaded with bricks. He was now dressed in a blue leather motorcycle suit with black stripes on its shoulders. Aztec walked over to the pool table that the D-boys surrounded, and dumped both contents of the pillowcases upon it. The D-boys glanced at the stacks of dead presidents and drugs, but they didn't dare reach for any of it.

"I can't believe y'all niggaz, man! Y'all gon' let these niggaz and this mothafucking wetback come here, and do me like this? Me? King Midas! I put the golden touch on all of you niggaz and made you somebody when you weren't shit! You niggaz owe me! You owe me witcha ungrateful, disloyal, trifling, scandalous, black hearted asses!" King Midas danced at the end of the rope as he talked big shit. He harped up some bloody mucus and spat it across the basement. He hoped it would land on one of the D-boys, but it fell short. "I want chu mothafuckaz to remember me! I want chu to remember this face 'cause it's gonna haunt cho black asses for the rest of your—"

King Midas was cut short by the three punch combination that La'Quan dropped on him. The last punch landed against his jaw and whipped his head aside, making him spit blood.

"Shut the fuck up! Don't none of them wanna hear that shit!" La'Quan assured him angrily. "They made their choice, and you made yours. Now deal with what comes with that."

Click-Clack!

The sound of a gun being cocked drew La'Quan's attention over his shoulder, where he found Aztec's gloved hand holding a handgun with a silencer on it. Aztec, who had a toothpick at the corner of his mouth, motioned one of the D-boy's over and handed him the gun. Keeping his eyes on King Midas, he pointed at him and told the D-boy to shoot him. The D-boy did as he was ordered. The bullet whistled through the air and shattered the bone of King Midas's kneecap.

"Aaaaaaah!" King Midas threw his head back, screaming aloud with tears in his eyes, which eventually rolled over his temples.

"Alright, good job, now, you, come up here!" Aztec called out to a D-boy and motioned him over. He was wearing a du-rag, a hoodie and an oversized white T-shirt. Murtaugh placed the gun in his hand and directed him to shoot King Midas. The youth turned the gun sideways and pulled the trigger.

"Aaaaaah!" King Midas screamed in excruciating pain, feeling another hot bullet tear through his lower intestines. He had agony written all over his face. "Oh, oh, shit! I'm bleeding. I'm bleeding really badly, man. Stop, stop, I'll get with the program! I'll work under ya man, Joaquin!"

"Too-mothafucking-late, that offer has expired, gilipollas!" Aztec spat heatedly and motioned another one of the D-boys over to him. He handed him the gun and directed him to do what the last D-boy had done. He did, and King Midas's black-ass was screaming in pain again.

King Midas didn't stop getting popped until every D-boy in the basement had put a bullet in him. By the time they'd finished, King Midas was barely alive and breathing shallowly, eyes rolled to their whites, blood dripping on the floor.

Marquette, who had been in the cut of the basement the entire time, stepped before King Midas. He whipped out a pair of black leather gloves and pulled them over his hands, flexing his fingers inside of them. Pulling back the sleeve of his black leather suit, he looked at the time and then back up at King Midas. "Well, it's time we call it a night, Mr. Midas. Have fun in the next life." Marquette flashed him a sinister smile and waved goodbye to him. He stepped behind him and grabbed hold of the five gold rope chains around his neck, which were attached to some pretty heavy medallions. Clenching his jaws, Marquette pulled the five gold chains back against King Midas's throat with all of his might. King Midas's glassy eyes bulged, veins tensed on his forehead, and he started gagging. The gold rope chains had cut off his oxygen, and he was struggling to breathe. His body sporadically shook, as he fought for his life.

King Midas's movements grew slower and slower, as

his life force began to slip away. Shortly thereafter, he took his last breath and went limp on the rope. He shitted in his slacks, and a dark wet spot expanded at his crotch, urine dripping down to the floor. Having sent King Midas off to the afterlife, Marquette walked from behind him, wiping the beads of sweat from his forehead. Strangling King Midas proved to be strenuous work and definitely not quite easy as it looked in the movies.

"Alright, y'all listen up," Aztec began. While Marquette had busied himself strangling King Midas, he separated the money and the bricks into two neat stacks. "You're gonna be working under our boss now, and that comes with perks. My partners and I will turn over the drugs to our employer, but we'll split the money amongst you all. How's that sound?" The D-boys nodded their approval, and some of them clapped their hands. The others smiled and dapped each other up. They were all for getting free money. They'd never gotten any benefits under King Midas's reign.

Aztec handed out twenty grand each to the D-boys, making sure everyone saw a cut of King Midas's money. There were sixty gees left on the pool table, which Aztec, La'Quan and Marquette were going to split among themselves. Aztec put the bricks back inside of the pillowcase and handed one of the D-boys a card.

Holding the card between both hands, the D-boy read it over. Aztec told him it was where they were supposed to be, so they could start back working—for Joaquin.

"Enjoy those dead presidents, boys; don't spend it all at one place," La'Quan urged the D-boys. Once Aztec hoisted the pillowcase of bricks over his shoulder, they all followed behind him up the staircase.

Chapter 10

Compton
Burger King in the Compton Towne Shopping Center

Bankroll Benny was a thirty-one-year-old brother with skin the color of brass. He was rocking a sky-blue and red Chicago Bulls fitted cap, gold framed glasses, and a Scottie Pippen Chicago Bulls' basketball jersey that matched perfectly with his cap. A gold thirty-inch Cuban link chain hung around his neck. A large icy gold Christ the Redeemer statue pendant hung from it, its diamonds sparkling and shining. Bankroll Benny had an icy gold four finger ring on both his hands. One read 'Bankroll' and the other 'Benny'— which paid homage to his namesake.

Bankroll Benny was standing before ten of his workers, who were sitting down in front of him, consuming their meals and taking occasional sips from their fountain drinks. Their eyes were glued to him as he moved animatedly with his fountain drink. He was telling a story about a sticky situation he was in back in the day. A time that was way before he was the self-proclaimed Crack King.

"...So, me and this big ass nigga gets to struggling for control of the strap, right? Cocksucka head-butted me and I let it go. But then I realize, oh, shit, he's got the gun. This mothafucka gon' kill me, so I kick his big ass in his balls. I mean, I cock my leg all the way back and really let go on his ass like, boom!" Balling up his face and biting down on his bottom lip, he reenacted how hard he kicked his opponent in his dick and balls. His workers cringed and look away as some of them ate their food, imagining the pain the poor bastard must have felt from such a kick. "I got 'em up off me and I go for the gun. I guess he was like me, sensing his life was in danger. He shakes off the aching in his nuts and tackles me to the floor before I can get my hands on my blower. Next thang I know, we're squabbling like a mothafucka! I'm giving nem punches and haymakers, and he's giving them back. But what he's dropping on me is causing much more damage to me than my punches are causing to him, though. Shit, I'm five-foot-eight and one hundred and fifty-five pounds, while this big ol' sucka 'bout six-foot-three and two hundred and forty something pounds—"

"Yo, wait a minute, where this nigga Worm was at though? Why he didn't come help you?" one of Bankroll Benny's workers asked and took a bite of his Whopper. As soon as he did, a mixture of mustard and ketchup squirted out on his crisp white T-shirt. His face balled up annoyingly, and he looked down at it. "Fuck, bruh! I ain't gon' never get this mothafuckin' stain out!"

Bankroll Benny took another sip of his fountain drink, causing the straw to make that empty cup sound. He shook the cup back and forth and heard the ice cubes rattling inside of it. He adjusted the straw inside the cup and sucked what was left out of it. Balled fist to his mouth, he belched and passed the cup to one of his workers heading to the trash can to dump his tray. "Throw that away for me, School Boy," he told him. School Boy was a nerdy looking African American kid who wore glasses and a button-down shirt under a sweater vest. The youth looked like he spent most of his time with his face in a book. That wasn't the case at all with him, though. He spent most of his time slinging Bankroll Benny's poison. In fact, the boy was his top earner and his most valued employee. "Good looking out, my young nigga. What the fuck is this?" His forehead wrinkled, seeing the crumbs from the burger he'd eaten earlier on his shirt. He brushed the crumbs off. "But, yeah, back to what I was saying, I—"

Bankroll Benny found himself being interrupted again when his cell phone rang.

"Goddamn, man, who the fuck is this?" He pulled out his personal cell phone, but it wasn't the one ringing. That's when he realized it had to have been the cellular he conducted business on. He switched hands with his personal cell phone and pulled out the other. The entire time, his workers were waiting in suspense for him to finish the epic story he was telling them. They couldn't wait to find out what their homeboy Worm was doing while he was fighting with that big ass dude. "Who the hell is this?" Bankroll Benny wondered, as he looked at the 'Blocked Number' on the screen of his business phone. He didn't know who the fuck would be calling him from a blocked number. Figuring it was probably his side bitch; he went ahead and answered it. "What's up, lil' mama?" Bankroll Benny listened to what he was being told. His brows furrowed because he didn't like it. His workers, seeing the hostile expression on his face, exchanged concerned glances, wondering what was up. "You can take yo' business proposal and shove it up yo' funky ass, homeboy! Bankroll Benny and his product is a brand, furthermore, I'ma self-made man. A boss. Fuck I look like demoting myself to a worker? Nigga, kill yo'self!" He disconnected the call and turned around to his workers.

"Yo, Benny, everything good?" School Boy asked, while enjoying what was left of his fountain drink.

"Yeah, it's all good. Just some buster ass nigga hitting me up with some ol' bullsh—" The rest of Bankroll Benny's words died in his mouth, as rapid gunfire shattered the window behind him. He did a funny dance on his feet, as bullets wet his ass up from the outside, going through his front and coming out his back. Once the gunfire ceased, a horrified-looking Benny dropped to his knees, as wisps of smoke rose from the bloody holes of his body. Abruptly, he fell face down on the floor, and his blood slowly formed a pool beneath him.

Benny falling face down on the floor revealed a helmeted, black leather motorcycle suit-clad La'Quan and Marquette. They were both clutching suppressor-equipped Uzis with both hands, and smoke was wafting from them. In the background of them, there were their Ducati motorcycles lying propped against kickstands, one of which Aztec was mounted on. He wore a helmet and had a matching Uzi in his gloved hand. His neck was on a swivel as he was watching the streets for police presence.

Bankroll Benny's workers put their hands in the air, surrendering. Although they were strapped, La'Quan and Marquette already had the drop on them. La'Quan and Marquette pulled open the entrance door of Burger King. They made their way inside, with the broken glass from the shattered window crunching beneath their boots. Marquette looked to the counter where patrons went to place their orders. All of the Burger King employees were standing perfectly still with their hands up in the air. Some of them were so scared they were shaking.

"How many of y'all are back there?" Marquette asked the cashier. She was a black girl sporting heavy make-up, fake eyelashes, a forty-inch long weave and acrylic nails that looked like talons.

"Si—Six—" the cashier said nervously. She was visibly shaken, but she was trying to remain cool for fear of getting chopped down.

Marquette flipped open the visor of his helmet and walked up on the cashier. Leaning forward, he took a closer look at her name tag to see what it read.

"Jamaica, right?"

"Y—Yes," Jamaica stammered.

"Jamaica, I want chu to call your co-workers up here and tell 'em to lay down on their stomachs, with their fingers interlocked behind their heads, okay?" Marquette asked calmly. Jamaica nodded. "Okay, do that now," he told her, and she obliged him. The workers came from out of the kitchen and did exactly what they were told. Once they had, Marquette glanced over his shoulder at La'Quan. He'd just pulled out one of Joaquin's business cards, held it up for Bankroll Benny's workers to see, and then placed it gently on one of the table tops. He continued on to say something else to them that Marquette couldn't quite hear. The young killa had snatched up Jamaica and walked her to the back of the fast food restaurant to retrieve the DVD footage of Bankroll Benny's assassination. A minute later, Marquette was coming back with a disc.

"Gon' and lay down next to your co-workers with your fingers interlocked behind your head, Jamaica," Marquette told her as he held her at gun point and slipped the disc inside of his motorcycle suit. After Jamaica did what he'd instructed, he approached La'Quan and told him, 'I got it'. Together, they walked outside, mounted their Ducatis, and sped off. The sound of police car sirens filled the air.

***

Collette sat on the mattress in her bra and panties, antsy to get the crack pipe and lighter from Charlie, who was getting high as a kite. He held the blue flame of his lighter to the end of the crack pipe and sucked on the end of it, pulling smoke in his lungs. He took a few puffs of the glass dick and blew it out into the air, head tilted back, and eyelids narrowed into slits. He brought his head down, and passed the pipe and the lighter to Collette's awaiting hands. As soon as she got the lighter and the smoking utensil, she lit up. The first blast seemed to put her at ease. A pleased look came across her face. Her big, black chapped lips formed a smile. She put the pipe to her lips again and lit up, puffing long and strong, indulging in her poison of choice.

As smoke wafted around Collette, Charlie rose from off the mattress and started slipping on his socks and sweat-pants. Once he had them on, he tied up the drawstring to them and slipped a wife beater over his head. He then lifted up his pillow and grabbed the old, black six-shooter revolver that was lying there. The pistol looked like it was used to stick up banks in the western days. Charlie tucked his pistol in the front of his sweatpants and threw on a dingy green T-shirt. The last thing he put on was a pair of raggedy high-top Nikes with the orange basketball on the tongue of them. At this time, Collette was watching him closely, wondering where he was going.

"Where you headed, bae?" Collette asked nosily.

"That's the last of our stash you're smoking. I figure I'd get out here and make some moves to insure we have the capital for our next fix."

Collette sat the lighter and the crack pipe aside, crawling to the end of the mattress, where Charlie stood. Smiling, she tugged on his sweatpants and garnered his attention. He turned around to find Collette looking up at him.

She told him smilingly: "You know that's what I've always liked about chu, you're a go-getter. Now, gemme some lip." Charlie cracked a one-sided grin and kissed her passionately.

"Since you like how much of a go-getter I am, how about chu assist a brother on his mission?" Charlie said.

"You got it, boo, just lemme finish this lil' bit up." Collette held up the lighter and the crack pipe from where she was sitting on the mattress.

"Cool." Charlie plopped down upon the mattress. "You can listen to this plan I got that's gon' seal the deal on our next blast."

"I'm all ears, big daddy," Collette assured him, putting the crack pipe between her lips and igniting a flame to bring to its tip.

Thirty minutes later, Charlie and Collette were making their way out of the house and walking down the street. The plan they had in mind was as simple as two-plus-two. Collette was to go to a crack house and act like she was going to purchase a few rocks. As soon as whoever was working the door opened it to make the exchange, Charlie was going to kick the door in and make niggaz lay it down on the floor. He was going to clean the place of whatever drugs it had and make a fast getaway. Right that minute, he and Collette were on their way to procure a car for the night's mission.

Collette's forehead wrinkled worriedly, noticing a black van slowly crawling up the block behind her and Charlie. Discretely, she whispered in Charlie's ear to let him know her findings. He pretended like he was bending down to tie his sneaker and she acted like she was waiting for him. Sure enough, the van was right there creeping up on them like she'd said. Charlie stood upright and interlocked his fingers with Collette's, walking up the sidewalk, trying their best to appear oblivious to the lingering threat at their rear.

"Bae, you seen 'em?" Collette whispered to Charlie.

"Yeah, I seen them mothafuckaz—a white boy and an ese, they're definitely trying to creep on us. I gotta trick for their monkey-asses though." Charlie stared ahead. Slowly, he inched his hand toward the revolver concealed in his waistline, preparing to make his move. "Alright, look, on the count of three, I'ma turn around and light up that van. You take off running and dip inside of the alley, wait for me at the end of it. Okay?"

"Okay." Collette said, eyes watering. Tears broke down her cheeks, and she swiftly wiped them away.

"Gemme a kiss," Charlie demanded and she obliged. "Alright, on the count of three, we're gonna make our move."

Charlie and Collette counted to three. As soon as they reached three, Charlie whipped around and upped his pistol, pulling its trigger. Flames spat from the barrel and ripped through the windshield on the passenger side. By this time, Collette was darting across the street and disappearing inside of an alley.

Lowering his smoking revolver, Charlie darted across the street right on Collette's heels. As he closed the distance between himself and the alley, the van jumped the curb, speeding in his direction. *Boomp!* Charlie went upon the hood of the van and rolled down off of it, smacking down onto the asphalt. He lay flat on his back, wincing, and his pistol two feet away from him. Instantly, Hugo, wearing a ski mask over his face, threw open the passenger door and jumped down. He had a zip-tie in his hand and a tranquilizer gun in the other.

"Catch up to that bitch, I got this one!" Hugo told Murtaugh before slamming the passenger door shut.

The van sped down the alley Collette was making hurried footsteps through. Hugo upped his gun and fired a dart into Charlie's body, putting him to sleep almost instantly. As he snored, Hugo went right to work, flipping him over on his stomach and binding his wrists behind his back. Hugo took a quick scan of the block to make sure there wasn't anyone watching him. He pulled a black pillowcase from out of his back pocket and pulled it down over Charlie's head. He stuck the pistol he'd lost when he was hit inside of his pocket, and hoisted Charlie's limp body over his shoulder. Once again, Hugo scanned the area for any witnesses before making hurried footsteps up the alley.

***

A terrified look was on Collette's face as she huffed and puffed, running up the alley. Occasionally, she'd glance over her shoulder, seeing the black van getting closer and closer to her. Realizing it may catch up to her sooner than she expected, she cut across the alley and made to jump upon a gray bricked wall. The van skidded to a stop closely behind her, and the driver's door swung open. A masked up Murtaugh jumped out with a cattle-prod down at his side. He saw Collette holding onto the wall and attempting to bring her leg over it.

Before she could perform this action, Murtaugh ran over to her and pulled her down by the end of her jean jacket. Seeing she was about to fall, he stepped clear of her and she crashed down onto the trashy, graveled ground. As she lay wincing in pain, Murtaugh zapped her in the neck, which made her holler. Next, he pulled a syringe filled with a very powerful sedative from within his jacket, and snatched its cap off with his teeth. He spat the cap aside and kneeled down to Collette, stabbing her in the neck with it. Pressing down on the syringe's plunger, he watched as its contents worked its magic on her.

Slowly, the tension vanished from Collette's face, and she was fast asleep. Tossing the syringe aside, Murtaugh prepared his victim to be placed in the van, with the zip-tie and the black pillowcase. With a grunt, he hoisted her over his shoulder and carried her to the back of the van, where Hugo was already waiting for him. Murtaugh opened up the back double doors of the van and placed Collette inside. Hugo was right behind him, depositing Charlie. They slammed doors of the van shut and high-fived each other. Afterwards, they jumped back into the van and Murtaugh drove off.

***

The wheels of a shopping cart squeaked as Wilson pushed it down the cracked sidewalk. Singing and dancing, he made his way down his route. Every now and again, he'd stop to dig through resident garbage cans to collect recyclables. This was his daily routine. He'd get up every morning to collect cans, bottles and any other items people discarded that he could make a profit off of. Once he cashed in what he collected, he'd use his profits to purchase his drug of choice—crack cocaine.

Old Wilson was a Vietnam War veteran that suffered greatly from a severe brain injury and PTSD. The medicine his therapist prescribed him didn't do jack-shit to suppress the mental torture he experienced every day. But through what he believed was the grace of God, he found exactly what he needed to remedy him: alcohol and crack. His vices may not have cured him, but they sure as shit made his train wreck of a life much easier to deal with. As of now, Wilson had copped himself a bottle of Wild Turkey Kentucky Bourbon, and seven grams of crack cocaine he couldn't wait to smoke.

Wilson grabbed his bottle of Bourbon from his shopping cart, which was concealed inside a brown paper bag. He screwed off its top and took it to the head, Adam's apple moving up and down. After wiping his wet chin with the back of his gloved hand, he danced up on the passenger window of a parked Cutlass Supreme, singing to his reflection. Wilson was a five-foot-ten, seventy-two-year-old man who was in phenomenal shape, physically. He rocked a baldhead, but the cowlicks on either side of his head were still visible. He was a slender man with a nappy beard that was almost completely white.

Wilson took a few more drinks of the Wild Turkey before screwing its cap back on and placing it back inside of his shopping cart. He went to push the cart forward, but the whiff of something foul grabbed his attention. Holding up his right arm, Wilson turned his head toward his pit and took a few sniffs. His face wrinkled, as a putrid smell invaded his nostrils; so he brought his arm down.

"God damn, my ass is musty ass a polecat! I gotta get to the men's room and wash my black ass, shit!" Wilson said to no one in particular, and continued to push his shopping cart forward. He went right along, singing and collecting the recyclables.

Wilson had finally arrived at 109th street Recreational Center, where he'd often come to wash up. The man that ran the place gave him permission to use the facility's men's room whenever he needed. Wilson worked at the park, keeping the gymnasium and the grounds cleaned. So, he considered him being able to use the men's room as an added bonus.

Wilson pushed his shopping cart inside of the men's room, and was caught by surprise by the presence of another shopping cart. As he tried to recall who the shopping cart belonged to, he narrowed his eyelids, massaging his chin. Giving up on remembering, Wilson shrugged and began the task of removing his clothing. Once his upper half was naked, he grabbed the items he needed to take care of his hygiene, including a washcloth.

Singing, Wilson approached the sink and got his wash-cloth wet. Once he used it to wash his face and clean his ears, he took some soap from the dispenser to lather up. His entire upper body was masked in whiteness and had soap suds covering it. He started washing the soap from off him, when he heard the loud flush of a toilet. Shortly thereafter, an old white man came shambling out of the last stall, zipping up his jeans and buttoning them. He was balding at the top of his head, and had a graying scruffy beard. He had on a blue puffy jacket with the stuffing hanging out of the arm of it and the opposite shoulder of it. He wore an orange sweatshirt underneath it, and blue jeans with tears at their knees.

"Whew, boy, I feel ten pounds lighter," the old white man said to no one in particular. He rolled up the sleeves of his jacket and prepared to wash his hands. The men were so occupied by what they were doing that they hadn't noticed each other yet. A moment later, they both looked up into the mirror that stretched the entire length of the wall, mad-dogging each other through their reflections.

"Well, isn't it ol' puss-ass Beecher. I told you if I saw yo' cracka ass again that it was on sight, nigga! And I meant that!" Wilson dropped his washcloth and yanked a big ass knife from where it was sheathed at his back. The knife was so huge it looked bigger than him. A gleam swept up the length of it, and it twinkled at its tip. Hurriedly, the old white man, Beecher, dashed over to his shopping cart and rifled through the junk he'd collected. He grabbed the old brown leather sheath he kept his knife in, and pulled it free. Holding the knife up before his eyes, Beecher smiled wickedly and watched a gleam sweep up its length. He then whipped around to Wilson and showed it off, bragging.

"Mine is bigger than yours, punk-ass!" Beecher laughed and gave him a glimpse of his missing and rotten teeth.

"I'm gonna carve yo' ass up like a Thanksgiving turkey, Beecher! You fucking thief!" Wilson swore angrily, as he and Beecher circled one another, ready to spill each other's blood.

"I'm notta goddamn thief, you black son of a bitch!" Beecher barked, spit flying off his lips. He had white shit at the corners of his mouth, so he looked like a dog foaming at the grill.

Wilson and Beecher were old Vietnam War buddies who had been thrown away and forgotten by society. The two of them had been as thick as thieves since the war ended. They'd lost contact a few years later, but winded up linking back up in the streets, chasing money alongside each other to get the poisons of their choosing. Last week, after a long night of reminiscing and drinking, they fell asleep inside of Wilson's tent on Skid Row. When Wilson woke up the next morning, his secret stash of crack was gone, and old Beecher was long gone.

Beecher swore up and down that he hadn't stolen Wilson's stash. But he was lying like a mothafucka, and Wilson knew it. They'd bumped into each other at the recycling center a few weeks ago. Wilson was ready to put hands on him, but mutual friends stopped it from going down. That very day, Wilson swore on everything he loved that the next time he came across Beecher, he was getting at him on sight. And now, here they were, face to face.

Wilson and Beecher engaged in a knife fight. They went cut for cut, but the damage either one of them inflicted wasn't life-threatening. Eventually, Wilson gained the upper hand by kicking the knife out of Beecher's hand. He then head butted him and broke his nose. Following up, he slammed his knee into his balls and dropped him to his knees. Beecher croaked in agony and held himself with both hands. Fluidly, Wilson slipped behind him and pulled his head back by his chin. Beecher's Adam's apple was left exposed, and he was too weakened from his aching nut sack to defend himself. With Beecher at his mercy, Wilson pressed the tip of his knife to the other side of his neck and a bubble of blood formed. The bubble slid down the side of Beecher's neck. Wilson scowled and bit down on his bottom lip. He was about to drag the knife over Beecher's Adam's apple and to the other side of his neck.

Boom!

The men's room door swung open from a powerful kick and startled Wilson. Masked up, Murtaugh and Hugo rushed inside. Murtaugh was holding two black pillowcases and Hugo was holding a tranquilizer dart gun. Hugo upped the tranquilizer gun and pulled its trigger. The dart ripped through the air and stuck to Wilson's forehead. He went cock-eyed and fell on his back, fast asleep. Beecher rose up from him, rubbing his neck and looking back at him. He then turned around to the men, thanking them for saving his life.

Hugo pointed his tranquilizer gun at Beecher and pulled its trigger. Beecher attempted to scream, but the dart nailed him directly in his chest. Shortly, he fell asleep. Murtaugh moved in on him and Wilson. While Murtaugh went to prepare the old crackheads for transportation, Hugo went to retrieve the van. He backed it up as close to the men's room door as he could, and then he hopped out. Once he opened the back double doors of the van, he assisted Murtaugh with loading their newest captives inside of it.

"Man, this plan Joaquin put together is really the fuck

out there, but if it works then we stand to make a shit load of money off of it," Hugo said before he jumped down from the back of the van.

"You bet your ass we do." Murtaugh closed the double doors of the van, one by one. He and Hugo hopped into the van and pulled off their ski masks. Murtaugh resurrected the van and pulled off like they just didn't kidnap a couple of crackfiends.

"How many more of these fucking smokers do we have to get?" Hugo asked Murtaugh, before he took the time to spark up a cigarette. He blew smoke out of the passenger window and then took the square out of his mouth.

"Three more, and then we move on to the next phase of the plan," Murtaugh answered. "Procure the product, open up the kitchen, and start cooking so we can get to this money."

"Yeah, that's what I'm talking about." Hugo smiled and dapped up Murtaugh.

Chapter 11

Buzzzzzz!

The iron gate with the barbed wire on top of it rolled back. A moment later, Zeus strolled out with a brown paper bag tucked under his arm. He was dressed in a blue Dickie short sleeve shirt, shorts, and All Star Chuck Taylor Converses. Black sunglasses shielded his eyes from the blazing hot sun, which was shining down upon him, making his shiny bald head gleam. He looked up at it, wincing, thinking, *Goddamn, Cuz, it's hot as a mothafucka out here! The Loc coulda never beena slave picking cotton out the field.*

Feeling two beads of sweat sliding down the side of his face, Zeus pulled his blue bandana from his left back pocket and dabbed his sweaty face dry. He then started in the direction of Joaquin's whip. Joaquin was sitting behind the wheel, looking like he was enjoying the air conditioner. Zeus couldn't wait to hop into his homeboy's ride and feel that cold A.C. blowing against his bald head. It was sweltering temperatures like this that made a nigga really appreciate winters and shit.

Seeing his former crime partner approaching his vehicle, Joaquin grinned and pressed the button to automatically unlock the passenger door. Zeus grinned back at him as he met his reflection in the passenger window. He'd put on weight, gaining about twenty pounds since he'd been incarcerated on his unregistered firearm charge. Besides that, he looked as much the same as he did when he first entered between the walls of The Beast. Zeus was thirty years old and weighed two-hundred-and-thirty-five pounds. He stood a whopping six-foot-two, and was built like a young Arnold Schwarzenegger.

Zeus had gotten his name based on his size and the

strength behind his punches. It was said that getting hit by him was the equivalent of getting struck by lightning, and everyone he'd fought could attest to that.

Zeus snatched open the passenger door and slid onto the front passenger seat, slamming the door behind him. The cold air the air conditioning provided welcomed him with open arms, and a look of relief came across his face. Zeus and Joaquin exchanged *'What's ups?'* and dapped up. The two men used to hit licks together back in the day, but they eventually went down their separate paths. Joaquin tried his hand at the murder-for-hire game, while Zeus and his pack of hungry dogs stuck to robberies and the extortion of drug dealers. They both found ghetto fame and fortune in their respective trades.

Although they weren't getting money together like they used to, every now and again Zeus and Joaquin would throw each other a lick here and there for old times' sake. That camaraderie was the reason Joaquin was here picking him up now. He knew that his homeboy was always looking for a way to make some cash, and he had just the opportunity for him.

"How does it feel to be home?" Joaquin asked Zeus, as he made sure there weren't any oncoming cars before pulling out into traffic.

"Real good, man, real good. You got some smoke in here?" Zeus inquired. He was blowing big weed while he was locked up; so, naturally, he was fiending to get high again.

"Yeah, I got half of a lil' something left. It's in this tray, hold up." He fished the half-smoked blunt from out of the ashtray, fired it up and passed it to Zeus. Zeus let the passenger seat backwards before indulging in the bleezy and blowing clouds of smoke.

"Check this out, my nigga," Joaquin began. "I gotta bag for you since you just came home, and I'ma take you shopping and the whole nine. But I gotta 'notha check for you if you're willing to do some wet work for me." *'Wet work'* meant he wanted Zeus to kill some niggaz.

Zeus blew out smoke from his nose and mouth before replying. "I'm hungry, my nigga. You set a meal down in front of me and a nigga gon' eat. You feel me?"

"My nigga, that's what I like to hear," Joaquin smiled. "Here's what I want chu to do—" he ran down to him what he wanted done.

"Cuz, wetting up shit is my specialty, so you came to the right nigga. I'ma need some help with this shit though, I'ma needa bring in the team?"

"Whatever you need, my nigga, money isn't an object."

Zeus nodded and said, "Alright, alright, how much are we talking here?"

"How many you bringing on for the job?"

"Ummm, Danja, Eat 'em Up, Bird, Crypto and Crip Walk," he counted off on his fingers, "'bout five."

"Okay, how does forty apiece sound?"

"Lovely."

"Alright. Gather you troops so we can get the ball on this shit rolling."

"I got chu faded, don't even worry about it," Zeus told him. "Lemme see yo' cell, big dog."

As soon as Zeus got Joaquin's cell phone, he hit up his crew to let them know he was as free as a bird and had a lucrative situation for them.

***

A couple of days later

The sun was shining brightly. Although the sky was partially cloudy, it was exceptionally warm. The day was stunningly beautiful, perhaps too beautiful for a funeral to be taking place. Inside of the chapel was packed. In fact, it was so packed that people were standing up because there wasn't any place to sit. There were many people that loved Asad, in and out of the streets. But a great amount of people attending the funeral were there because of God. They were either street niggaz who he conducted business with, or some little niggaz trying to gain favor with him.

God, Country and Buck Wild posted up against the wall. They were dressed in tailored suits that fit them to perfection. God was the only one rocking shades out of the three of them. One may think it was because of the beaming sun, but it was really due to the fact he'd been crying a lot that day. It was like he couldn't help himself. The tears kept falling and falling. He found himself ducking off to the men's room, or a far corner numerous times, to dab his eyes. It wasn't so much so that he was ashamed of someone seeing him cry. It was the fact that some of his acquaintances would see his tears as a weakness. They'd then think he was vulnerable, and may try to make a move on the operation he'd firmly established. He already had Joaquin and his goons to deal with. He sure as hell wasn't trying to add more enemies to his shit list, at least not while his head wasn't on straight.

Though Billie wanted to come to the funeral to support him, God insisted that she stay behind with the girls. He didn't want them seeing Asad lying in a casket. He believed seeing a loved one dead could fuck a child up mentally. He'd seen many of his homeboys before they were put to rest, and the way they looked his last time seeing them haunted him every day of his life. If he could help it, he never wanted to expose the girls to that. He wanted them to be of an age where they could understand the meaning between life and death. Right now he was sure they weren't; well, he was at least sure that Charity wasn't. He couldn't say for sure for Annabelle. He was still learning her, and didn't know of everything she'd been privy to.

Ammura was able to view Asad's body, and she was happy with the job that had been done on him. They had managed to sew his severed head and his severed limbs back together for him to have an open-casket ceremony. And the make-up artist had done such a fantastic job on his face that he appeared as if he was asleep. He was fitted in a gold tie and a white suit. He was wearing gold diamond earrings and a plain-faced gold Rolex. While the fluffy bedding of the casket was gold, the casket itself was white with gold handles. After the viewing of Asad's body, he was to be loaded inside a carriage, and white horses were to carry him to his burial site. Street veterans, niggaz who were lucky enough to survive the horrors that the street life brought, were to perform a twenty-one gun salute and then Asad would finally be lowered into the ground, his last resting place.

"Goddamn, Asad—" God shook his head, thinking it was a shame his young homie died so young. "Goddamn, man. I shoulda—I shoulda let somebody else handle things," he said to no one in particular as tears slid down his cheeks unevenly. Swiftly, he wiped the tears away with his curled finger and sniffled.

Buck Wild frowned up and looked at him. "You good, my nigga?" he asked, concerned.

God nodded and said, "Yeah. I'm straight. I'm good." He assured him with a fake smile.

Buck Wild nodded, but he knew that God wasn't okay.

Still, he wasn't going to press him any further. He'd much rather leave things as they were, and trust that he'd come to him if he wanted to chop it up. Buck Wild hung an arm on Country and God's shoulders.

"I love y'all two niggaz, man," Buck Wild told them.

"Love you too, dog," God told him.

"Shawty, you can't be just professing yo' love for a nigga and shit. You've got to prove it, ya heard me?" Country glanced at him.

"How?" Buck Wild asked curiously with a wrinkled forehead.

"You gon' have to sucka nigga dizniyee or something, big homie," Country replied with a gold grill smile.

"Man, I'm 'bouta kill this nigga." Buck Wild cracked a grin and turned to Country throwing playful punches at him. Country chuckled and flashed his gold grill, which glinted.

"Shhhhhh!" An old African American lady hushed them, holding her finger to her lipstick-painted lips. She was the color of a copper-penny, with black moles at the corners of either of her eyes. She was wearing a big black hat and a matching black dress that stopped above her knees.

Buck Wild and Country quickly straightened out as they were chastised by the elderly woman.

Buck Wild cleared his throat with his fist to his mouth and said, "Sorry about that, Mrs. Evans."

"You two niggaz are too big to be causing all that ruckus in the house of Almighty God. You oughta be ashamed of yourselves." Mrs. Evans gave them the evil eye. If looks could kill, Buck Wild and Country would have dropped dead on the spot.

"Man, who this old ass broad think she's talking to?" an angered Country asked God in a hushed tone. "She must not know a nigga is a straight up killa in the field. I'ma have to make her senile wrinkled ass realize the pedigree of a nigga such as myself, shawty."

"Yo, calm yo' big country ass down, nigga," God told him in a hushed tone. "That's Asad's great auntie. Show some respect."

"Show some respect? Nigga, please, that bitch needa show me some respect," Country told him furiously. He was a second from pulling out his gun and raising hell in the House of God.

"Look, I'ma 'bouta take this big guerilla outside and chief one so he can calm down. We'll be right back. Hit my jack when it's time to view the body." Buck Wild threw his arm around Country's shoulders and led him toward the doors of the chapel. He pulled an already rolled blunt from inside of his suit and stuck it between his lips.

"Yo, cuzzo, where the fuck we going, bruh?" Country asked, agitated. He was still hot about Mrs. Evans old ass coming at him like he wasn't a certified head busta.

"To blow down this bleezy, country man, yo' black ass needa relax obviously," Buck Wild told him as he patted himself down for his lighter.

God looked at his two best friends, smirking and shaking his head. He loved those two crazy ass niggaz to death. He knew if it wasn't for them, he wouldn't have leveled up like he had in the crack game. Hell, he probably wouldn't be alive for that matter. He felt like he owed them a lot. And once they crushed Joaquin, he was going to make sure they lived like kings.

***

Zeus, Bird, Danja, Eat 'em Up and Crypto, who were wearing bullet-proof vests underneath their baggy clothing, rode in the back of the van, click-clacking and loading them thangz with blue bandanas. They kept a smoldering blunt in rotation among them. They were also silent. In fact, the only thing that could be heard among the four of them—as their homeboy, Crip Walk, drove the van—is Nipsey Hussle's "I Don't Give a Fucc".

My mama wanna know why I'm bangin'
She told me I'ma lose my life
I ain't trippin', I'm a crip and I'ma do it right
'Fore I run from a nigga I'll lose the fight...

"Aye, Cuz, turn that Nip up," Eat 'em Up said from the front passenger seat where he had his machine gun resting between his legs. He wouldn't be hopping out with the rest of the killaz. He'd stay behind in the van to act as backup, along with another one of the homies.

"Yeah, cuz, turn that shit up," Zeus chimed in, as he adjusted the drum on his machine gun. Crip Walk turned the volume up. Zeus nodded to the hypnotizing beat and lyrics, mentally preparing himself for the drama that was about to occur. He'd been in many firefights, all of which he came out on the winning end in, but he wasn't anyone's fool. He knew that every dog had its day. And today could very well be his day. "Yeah, that's it, Cuz. Good looking out." He locked and loaded his machine gun with deadly ammunition.

"This shit goes hard," Bird nodded and blew out a big cloud of smoke.

"Hell yeah, I used to listen to Cuz all the time while I was locked up," Crypto claimed, as he recovered the blunt from Bird.

While this was going on, Danja was taking a bottle of Hennessy to the head. When he brought the bottle down from his lips, he wiped his dripping mouth with the back of his hand and hissed, feeling the fiery liquid coat his throat and belly. He passed the bottle to Zeus. "Here you go," he told him.

"Good looking out, Cuz," Zeus said, after gulping the rest of the Hennessy, enjoying the effects of the alcohol.

Danja focused his attention back on his machine gun, smacking in the fully loaded clip and cocking that bitch. Once he'd done that, he kissed the deadly weapon and started loading slugs inside of the extra magazines he'd brought along.

Once all the homies were locked and loaded, they pulled navy blue ski masks down over their faces and adjusted them so they could see out of their eyeholes. They then held hands and bowed their heads in prayer.

"Lord, make us fast and accurate. Let our aim be true and our hand faster than those that we seek to kill. Grant us a victory over our enemies and those that wish to do harm to us. Amen!" the Crips said altogether. They then gripped their machine guns and prepared to jump out.

***

Country and Buck Wild posted up outside the chapel, joking and laughing while passing a blunt between them. They were so caught up in their conversation that they were ignorant of the van carrying the hit-squad of Crips intended to take out God and everyone else in attendance at the funeral. The van parked at the back of the chapel. Zeus, Bird and Crypto jumped out clutching their guns and looking about, making sure there wasn't anybody watching them. Having made sure the coast was clear, the trio moved in on the backdoor. Zeus and Crypto watched Bird's back as she picked the lock of the back door. Once it clicked open, she picked her gun and snuck her way inside. Zeus and Crypto followed her, as cautiously and quiet as they could. The further they proceeded down the hallway, the louder and clearer the minister's voice became.

Zeus, Bird and Crypto spilled out into the foyer where the funeral was taking place. When the ministers and the mourners saw them, they looked distraught and worried. They didn't know what the fuck was going on! Zeus, Bird and Crypto scowled behind their ski masks and clenched their teeth, lifting up their weapons, swaying them back and forth across the pews. The mourners screamed and hollered in agony as bullets chopped them down and splattered their blood on those gathered around them.

"Take out God!" Zeus ordered Crypto with the motion of his gloved hand in God's direction. As soon as they started firing, God had grabbed hold of Ammura—who was holding her sobbing daughter, rushing them to safety. He occasionally turned around to let his gun talk, keeping the opposition at bay.

"Gaaaah!" one of the mourners went down.

"Aaaaaah!" one of God's angels hit the floor next.

God disappeared down another hallway with Ammura and her daughter. Locating the women's rest room door, he opened it and escorted her and her baby girl inside. He then pulled out a .38 special from the ankle holster strapped to his leg and handed it to Ammura. Quickly, he showed her how to fire it. "You got it? Can you remember that?"

"Yes, yes, I got it! I'll remember it!" Ammura assured him. She held the gun in one hand while trying to get her baby girl to quiet down.

"Good. If any mothafucka comes through this door isn't me or the niggaz you seen me with, you squeeze that bitch on 'em 'til its empty! You got that?" Ammura nodded understandingly. "Alright, lock this door behind me!" God said, as he left the women's rest room. He started to walk out into the hallway, and Crypto sent a bullet his way, knocking a chunk out of the corner of the wall. God whipped his head back and narrowed his eyelids, to stop the debris masking the air from getting into his eyes. Listening closely, he could hear Crypto's footsteps as he slowly came his way, the sounds of gunfire behind him.

God looked down at the carpeted floor and saw Crypto's shadow as he eased closer to him. Clutching his gun with both hands, he looked back and forth between his gun and Crypto's shadow, trying to figure out what his next move was going to be.

Fuck this! This nigga not finna have me hiding like some mothafucking punk, God thought with a scowl. He spun off the wall and came out of the corridor, lifting his gun to fire. Crypto had lifted his gun with intentions of firing at him as well. He was about to pull his trigger when two different sets of gunshots erupted, their deafening sounds bouncing off the walls of the hallway. Crypto threw his head back, screaming in excruciation as bullets ripped through his back and splattered out of his front. Crypto clenched his teeth to fight back the agony from being shot. He then spun around to take a shot at the men that had pumped him full of holes.

Before Crypto could release a bullet in his threats' direction, they were chopping him down and sending him to his bloody death. He fell up against the wall and slid down to the carpeted floor. He sat up with his head tilted to the side and his hand still clutching his gun. His eyes were bulged and his mouth was hanging open, blood flowing fluidly from the corner of his lips.

God cautiously moved in on Crypto. He kicked his gun out of his hand, then kicked his leg. When he didn't budge, he placed two fingers to his neck to check his pulse. He was as dead as he looked! God looked down the hallway and saw Buck Wild and Country holding smoking guns. He narrowed his eyelids at them and leaned forward. It looked like they were wearing gold body armor, with white ruffle skirts, gold gauntlets and large white feathered wings. The guns in their hands appeared to turn into shiny metal swords. It was like his homeboys had transformed into his angels—his guardian angels!

God blinked his eyes again and took a closer look at Buck Wild and Country. They seemed to transform back to their normal selves.

"You good, boss dog?" Buck Wild asked God.

"Yeah, good looking out," God told him and tapped his fist against his chest.

After Buck Wild confirmed that God was straight, him, God and Country ran back into the foyer, trading bullets with Bird. They weren't any match for the firepower backing her, so they dispersed and hid behind a row of pews. Right after, Bird caught two in the chest which made her grimace. Looking over her shoulder and seeing the podium as a safe haven, she ran toward it, firing her machine gun at the opposition blindly.

Meanwhile, Zeus charged toward Asad's gold casket and kicked it with all of his might. The casket flipped over and dumped the young man's lifeless body onto the carpeted floor. Zeus, clutching his machine gun with both hands, ran up on Asad's carcass and pointed his automatic weapon at it. He held back its trigger, and the barrel of his machine gun flickered flames. Asad's body looked like it was break-dancing on the floor as it was torn apart by rapid gunfire.

"Nooooooo!" God, Buck Wild and Country called out in emotional torment, seeing Asad's body being desecrated. They pointed their guns at Zeus and started busting at him.

Zeus ducked for cover and whipped around fast. He pulled the trigger of his machine gun and sent fire their way again. God, Buck Wild and Country hid behind the pews again to reload their blowers. Zeus, being the savage he was, machine-gunned Asad's head from off his shoulders. He then picked it up and kicked it across the chapel. It deflected off the wall and rolled across the floor.

"Mothafuuuckaaaaaa!" Ammura screamed in a rage, with tears sliding down her cheeks. She upped her .38 special and pulled its trigger, back to back. The chamber of the pistol twisted, and fire ignited its barrel time and time again.

Blam, blam, blam, blam!

The slugs slammed into Zeus' body, propelling him backward until he was off his feet. In free fall, he pointed his machine gun at Ammura and pulled its trigger. Rapid gunfire struck her torso and traveled upward, tearing holes in her chest, neck, and obliterating her head. Bloody pieces of her face, skull and chunks of brain matter went flying everywhere. Ammura dropped to her knees and fell flat on her face.

Zeus winced, as he lay on the carpeted floor, thinking how thankful he was to have worn a bullet-proof vest. Seeing people running back and forth across his line of vision, and God's angels reloading their guns to get at him, Zeus searched amidst the chaos for somewhere to take refuge. Right then, he saw Minister Jenkins who had been giving the sermon earlier running in his direction. A terrified look was on his face as he was heading to the hallway, where the back door was located. Zeus hurriedly scrambled to his feet and grabbed Minister Jenkins by the back of his suit's collar, yanking him into him.

"Come here, old man!" Zeus gritted, holding onto Minister Jenkins, with plans to use him as a human shield.

At this time, he saw the angels lifting their guns in his direction. Swiftly, he swung Minister Jenkins around in front of him just in time to take the bullets that were meant for him.

Splocka, splocka, splocka, blocka, blocka, blocka!
Bloc, bloc, bloc, poc, poc, poc, blowl, blowl, blowl!

"Aaaaaaaah!" Minister Jenkins screamed aloud, as a wave of bullets tore through his body, making it look like he'd been hit with a flurry of rotten tomatoes. After Minister Jenkins had slumped in Zeus' grip, he slung his lifeless body aside and upped his machine gun. He swept his machine gun across the angels. Some of them dove out of the way to avoid the onslaught, but there were others that weren't as fortunate. They, however, were mutilated by piping hot lead. As soon as they were cut down by gunfire, they fell to their deaths.

"Aye, Cuz, it's getting hot in here, you've gotta bail us out! I'm sure if we make a run for it we'll be cut down!" Bird spoke into her ear-bud as she sprayed the angels with her machine gun.

"I'm onnit, loc," Crip Walk responded from over the ear-bud.

"Now, nigga, now!" Bird shouted over the sounds of gunfire, where she'd taken cover behind the bullet-riddled podium, reloading her machine gun. While she was doing this, bullets were flying from every direction. Some of them struck the wall in front of her, while others slammed into the podium and sent splinters flying everywhere.

Bird narrowed her eyes into slits to stop debris from getting in them. She then poked her head out from behind the podium to see some of God's angels reloading their heat. A couple of them started to raise their guns to fire, so she went to get off them before they could. She managed to drop one and hit another high in the thigh and kneecap. He hollered in agony and collapsed to the floor. Two of his homeboys held her at back with gunfire, while another one hastily dragged him out the chapel by the collar of his sweatshirt.

Screeeech! Vrooooom!

Ba-boom!

The back of the van crashed through the chapel, causing debris to fill the air and broken plaster to spill onto the carpeted floor. The double doors of the van opened and Danja, wearing a navy blue ski mask, jumped down onto the floor, with a machine gun.

"Ya'll niggaz come on, Cuz!" Danja called out to his comrades and motioned for them to pile up inside of the van. Zeus and Bird ran past Danja and climbed inside of the van. Once the last of his comrades had ran past him, Danja sprayed some of the angels. He managed to lay a couple of them down, while others were lucky enough to get arm and leg wounds.

While this was going on, God, Buck Wild and Country peeked out from behind the pews where they'd taken cover from Zeus' gunfire. When God laid his weary eyes on Ammura's body, his eyes filled with tears and his face twisted into a mask of hatred. Tears slid down his cheeks and he clenched his jaws, gripping his gun tighter.

"Let's get these mothafuckaz!" God said to Buck Wild and Country. They were just as hurt and angry as he was. Together, they came from behind the pews ready to claim as many lives of the Crips as they could. Danja was ignorant of them starting to make their move as he was busy reloading his machine gun. He ejected the magazine out of his automatic weapon and went to smack another into the bottom of it. But before he could carry out what he had in mind, God, Buck Wild and Country charged at him, letting their guns act a goddamn fool!

Blocka, blocka, blocka, blocka, blocka!

Boc, boc, boc, boc, boc!

Bloc, bloc, bloc, bloc!

God, Buck Wild and Country gunned Danja down. As he lay on the floor bleeding from every hole in his body, they ran up on him and kept firing, mutilating his face and body. The boy would be unrecognizable to even his mother. Seeing her comrade slaughtered, Bird had it in mind to jump out the van and get busy with God, Buck Wild, Country and the rest of the angels that were coming with their guns to aid them. She was about to hop out of the back of the van and let them have it, but Zeus yanked her ass back in.

"Are you fucking crazy, girl? Danja's dead! That nigga'z gone! And I'm not 'bouta sit up here and let chu go out with 'em." Zeus barked at her and slammed one of the double doors closed. As soon as he did, a wave of bullets slammed into the door, putting nickel sized holes in it. "Crip Walk, Cuz, pull off, pull off!"

Urrrrk!

The van sped out of the chapel with one of the back doors swinging from left to right. God, Buck Wild and Country chased behind the bullet-hole-riddled van, popping at it. Bullets deflected off the van's metal bumper and some of them slammed into the van itself. God, Buck Wild and Country lowered their guns. They then ran back inside of the chapel, their eyes were wide and their mouths were hanging open, looking around at all of the dead bodies littering the floor. The smell of blood and gun smoke lingered in the air like the stench from a fart.

There were whimpers and cries among the wounded and the loved ones of those who'd been slain. But there was one person's crying that stood out amongst them all—Aziza's.

The sight God witnessed when he turned around was enough to make even a gangsta cry. Instantly, his eyes filled with tears and they spilled down his face. Aziza was on her knees at her dead mother Ammura's body, tears flowing consistently down her face and splashing onto that of her mother's.

"Mommy, wake up—please, wake up! Don't leave me, mommy." Aziza begged as she shook her mother to get up. "Please, don't leave me—please don't leave me like daddy did. I—I don't wanna be alone. I—I promise I'll be good, and do whatever you say—just please, please don't leave me." Aziza gave up trying to wake her mother up. She sniffled and wiped her dripping eyes with her little fist. Leaning over, she brushed her mother's eyelids shut and kissed her affectionately on the cheek. She then snuggled up next to her and pulled her limp arm around her. Aziza shut her eyes and whimpered while in her mother's arm, trembling with overwhelming sadness.

"Damn, man," Buck Wild said sadly. Seeing Aziza like that with her mother fucked him up too. His eyes watered, and he blinked back tears. He then pulled a pair of black leather gloves on to his hands, making sure they were on firmly.

Country shook his head in pity of what had happened to Ammura, hating her daughter had to see her dead like that. He crossed himself in the sign of the crucifix.

God was walking over to Aziza to console her when Buck Wild ran over to him, stopping him with his hand to his chest. "Say, big dog, maybe you should give her some time alone with her mother—I think it's for the best." God nodded understandingly. "Gemme yo' blower too. The Boys coming and we gotta get rid of it." He extended his open palm to him, and God passed his piece to him. "Country, come on!" Buck Wild motioned for Country, who was sliding on a pair of gloves also, to follow him, as he ran toward the hole in the wall the Crips getaway van had created. Country made hurried footsteps behind him, police car sirens wailing as they sped to their location.

Keeping his eyes on Aziza, God sulked over to the damaged podium and sat down with his back to it. He leaned his head back against it, as he continued to watch Aziza weep. He stared up at the ceiling, as his eyes filled with tears again. He shut his eyelids, and wetness jetted down his cheeks.

I'm sorry, Asad. I'm really, really sorry, lil' bro, I fucked up—I fucked up, God thought as he brought his knees to his chest, rested his elbows on them and bowed his head. More tears coated his cheeks and slid off his chin, splashing on the carpeted floor.

Police officers cautiously moved inside of the chapel with their guns drawn, looking around for any one that may pose a threat to them. God knew they were there, but he ignored them. He continued to grieve over the loss of Asad's fiancée, feeling like he'd failed to protect her. His shoulders rocked, and tears continuously slicked his cheeks.

Chapter 12

That night

Zeus and his crew had parked the getaway van inside of an alley behind an old factory and torched it. Hugo picked them up in a van he'd rented, paid them for the massacre at the funeral, and drove them to a location of their choosing. Although they hadn't successfully killed God, Joaquin was good with paying them because he felt they'd sent a clear message to the kingpin: *Don't fuck with Joaquin!*

The basement was dark, save for the lone light bulb dangling from the string above the table. Its one-hundred-watt bulb illuminated mostly everyone gathered below it. Crip Walk, Bird and Eat 'em Up watched Zeus run the racks through a money-counter. Zeus dipped his hand in and out of a duffle bag. He'd pop the rubber band on the racks and drop them into the machine. He'd then sit back and watch the money-counter do its job, rapidly shuffling though the blue faces. Once it was done, Zeus would repeat this procedure. The money he was counting up was the loot that Joaquin had paid them to wet up Asad's funeral. Although they couldn't confirm they'd killed God, Zeus was pretty sure that they had, seeing as how they'd murked fifteen to twenty of God's killaz, and a couple civilians. Zeus figured that God had gotten caught up in the lot that they'd smoked. And he was going to be paying very close attention to the news over these next few days to see if his name and face popped up. If not, then he and his killaz were going to see to it that his mark-ass was dead once and for all.

"That's one hunnit and sixty bands, so that's forty geez apiece," Zeus announced, once the machine finished counting the racks. Afterwards, he separated the money for each individual in his crew. He stacked the racks neatly on top of each other and pushed them in front of the man and woman that made up his crew.

Everyone whipped out their sacks and pulled their earnings into them, dropping it off into their sacks. They then pulled the drawstrings on them and set them aside.

"So, what's next for us, Cuz?" Bird asked before taking the time to light up a cigarette. She took a few drags of it and blew out a big cloud of smoke, which slowly vanished within the atmosphere.

"I've gotta few things lined up but they aren't about shit," Zeus admitted, as he removed the wrapper from a blue berry Tootsie Roll sucker and placed it inside his mouth. He sucked on it for a minute before finishing what he had to say. "They'd pay even less than this caper we pulled off tonight."

"Shit, I ain't tripping of that—I got hella mouths to feed, so I'm always looking for the next gig that's gon' put food on the table, ya dig?" Crip Walk said, as he leaned back and forth in his chair, fondling the platinum dog tags of his necklace. There were a total of six of them with each of his children's face branded on them. Homeboy loved his kids to death, which is why he took penitentiary chances to make sure them and their mothers didn't want for anything.

Right then, a cell phone rang and vibrated, and everyone looked at Bird. Her brows furrowed because she hadn't brought her cellular along with her. She hadn't because she knew that law enforcement could use the towers to pinpoint where she was at during the funeral home massacre. Pulling the device from out of her pocket, she realized it was Hugo's cell phone she had. She'd asked to use it, and had forgotten to give it back to him.

"Yo, ain't that that Mexican dude's jack?" a frowning Eat 'em Up asked.

"Yeah, I forgot to give it back to 'em. I think this him right now. Hold on. Hello?" Bird answered the call, holding the cell phone to her ear. "What's up? Yeah, I got it. I'll meet chu outside to give it to you. Okay." She disconnected the call and rose from the chair, snatching up her sack. "Yo, I'm finna raise up. Homeboy is outside. I'ma give 'em his phone back and I'ma dip to the house. We'll talk business another time. A bitch tired as fuck, cuz."

Bird went around the table, dapping up her homeboys before heading up the staircase. The rest of the crips started back up, talking again, when they heard a loud and furious report of a shotgun.

Bloom!

A second later, Bird tumbled hard down the staircase and slid across the floor on her back. Her eyes were big and her mouth was wide open. A big bloody wound was on her chest that looked like ground up hamburger meat. She was dead!

Seeing their homegirl dead, the crips instantly went to grab their guns. They'd just cleared them from their waistline when a masked up Country hurried down the steps. He stopped at the halfway mark, lifted his shotgun, and opened fire again. The first blast flipped Eat 'em Up over the table, and he landed on the floor, sending some of the stacks of money high into the air. Crip Walk was about to extend his gun at Country and pull its trigger, but he wasn't fast enough. Country had already racked his shotgun for the third time and sent heat his way. Crip Walk flew backward, knocking over the chair beside him and slamming up against the wall. Wearing a dead expression on his face, Crip Walk slid down the wall and left a bloody smear behind. Zeus threw his sack of money at Country and it knocked his shotgun from out of his path. The shotgun went off and blew a chunk out of the brick wall, debris clouding the air.

By the time Country swung his shotgun back around, Zeus was already opening up on his big ass, pulling his trigger back to back. His bullets ripped through the air, shredding the fabric of Country's valor sweat suit and mashing against the bullet-proof vest he was wearing. Country gritted his teeth, feeling the strong impacts of the slugs. His gold teeth bit down onto his bottom lip to fight the pain in his chest. Steadying his shotgun on Zeus, he pulled its trigger twice which spun him around like a ballerina on ice skates. Country pulled the trigger of his shotgun a third time, and it lifted Zeus out of one of his sneakers. A pained look was on his face as he flew across the basement, slamming up against the door of the furnace and then smacking face first into the floor.

"Uhhhhh!" Zeus moaned and groaned, as he pushed himself up from the floor, blood dripping from his wounds and splashing on the floor. He looked up at Country and saw blurry double of him as he approached with his smoking shotgun. Although he was weakened from his wounds, Zeus summoned what little strength in him he had left and reached inside of his tattered jacket. When his hand came back out, he was holding a hunting knife, which gleamed and twinkled at its curved tip. "Come on, big boy, put the gun down and let's dance," he told him as a slither of blood spilled from the corner of his mouth. He licked it away and got into a fighting stance with his blade.

Country's black ass smiled devilishly and showcased that shiny gold grill. He had always been one for a challenge, especially when the odds were in his favor. "My pleasure—" Country retorted and tossed his shotgun aside. He then pulled a hunting knife similar to the one Zeus had from his valor sweat suit. It also gleamed. "I'ma carve yo' big black-ass up, shawty. Ya heard me?" He took a swipe at Zeus and opened a lengthy tear in his shirt. He then took a few more swipes at him, which he dodged. He followed up by thrusting his knife at his chest. Zeus hollered in agony and grabbed his chest, feeling the sharp metal pierce his skin. He looked to his hand and saw a smear of blood. His vision was fading in and out, so he knew he had to make short work out of the big country nigga. If not, he would surely be a dead man.

Grunting, Zeus launched an attack at Country, slicing up his shirt and leaving bloody cuts behind. Country came at him again, but he smacked his hand away. His hunting knife flew across the basement and slid across the floor, disappearing in between boxes. Zeus entangled his arm with Country's arm and pulled him close, slamming his forehead against his face and busting his nose. Blood sprayed out of Country's nostrils, and his eyes rolled back. He looked like he was about to faint. Seeing he had the upper hand, Zeus knew he had to act fast if he wanted to be victorious.

"You fucked with the wrong one, loc!" Zeus roared hatefully and swung the hunting knife downward. Right then, Country shoved a nickel plated .357 long barreled magnum revolver underneath his chin. Smiling wickedly, he pulled the trigger and blew Zeus' brains out the top of his skull. Blood droplets and brain fragments went high up in the air and splattered against the floor. Zeus wore a dead look on his face, as he dropped down to his knees and released his knife at his side. His knife clattered against the surface, and he fell, face down. Blood oozed out the gunshot wound at the top of his skull and slowly began to form a pool around it.

Country cocked back his leg and kicked Zeus hard as shit in his head. His forehead lifted up from the floor and smacked back down against it. He then harped up mucus and spat on Zeus' dead body.

"May you rest in shit!" Country told him. He moved to walk away, but then he felt something cold and hard placed against the back of his big bald head. He went rigid and stared out of the corner of his eyes. He didn't have to ask Hugo what he pressed against his dome because he already knew it was a gun.

"Drop the cuete, hijo de puta, or I'll drop you!" a scowling Hugo threatened. He wanted to take Country to Joaquin alive, but if he defied him he'd drop him right where he stood.

"Easy, big dog, you've got the upper hand here. It's yo' show, shawty." Country submitted. He dropped his pistol and slowly lifted his hands in the air, surrendering. Right then, unbeknownst to Hugo, Buck Wild crept upon him, holding his gun by its barrel. By the time Hugo felt his aura it was too late; he made to turn around, but Buck Wild was already whacking him across the back of his head. Instantly, Hugo dropped his gun and fell to the floor, out cold.

Country picked up his pistol and tucked it on his waistline. "It took yo' slow ass long enough. This spic was about to twist my cap back."

"Man, yo' ass too big to be whining like a lil' ass girl alla time," Buck Wild said, tucking his gun at the small of his back. He then pulled out a pair of handcuffs and clamped them around Hugo's wrists. "Help me lug his big ass up these stairs so we can put 'em in the trunk—Afterward, we gon' drench this bitch with gasoline and light it up," he told Country who had just returned from across the basement from recovering his hunting knife. He stashed it back where he'd pulled it from, and helped Buck Wild deposit Hugo inside of the truck. They grabbed the sacks of money. While Country went to load them inside of the car, Buck Wild went ahead and doused the entire basement in gasoline, leaving a trail down the steps. Next, he pulled out a box of matches, removed a stick and swept it across the black strip of the box. Holding the stick up, he admired its blue flame before tossing it on the flammable liquid. The entire house was engulfed in flames by the time he and Country were pulling away from the gruesome scene.

***

The old warehouse was massive, empty and extremely cold, thanks to the harsh winds and the heavy rain that had fallen earlier. Dirty droplets of water splashed on the wet graveled ground, while the occasional rat wandered about, sniffing around for anything that may be food. The supervisor's office sat high and far off into the right corner. Its lights were on. Two men—Country and Buck Wild—took turns pummeling Hugo who sat bound to an iron chair. When one of the men would find himself getting tired, the other would pick up where he left off, while he took drinks of bottled water and watched the show.

Country played the opposite side of the office, quenching his thirst while he watched Buck Wild rearrange Hugo's face with haymakers. Each of his devastating blows would knock a mixture of sweat and blood from the helpless Hugo, which would splatter against nearby file cabinets and the documents scattered on the floor. Once Buck Wild had grown exhausted with treating Hugo's face like a punching bag, he took a few steps back from him, placing his bloody gloved hands on his hips and tilting his head back. He took a couple of deep breaths, trying to calm himself down. Bringing his head back down, Buck Wild wiped the beads of sweat from his face with the sleeve of his shirt and turned around to Country, extending his hand.

"Yo', I'm fucking parched; toss me one of those waters, my nigga!" Buck Wild told Country, as he wiggled his fingers for one of the cold bottles of water. Country opened the small red and white cooler, digging his hand inside the pile of ice cubes. He pulled out a bottle of water and tossed it over to Buck Wild. Buck Wild quickly removed the cap off the bottle and guzzled down half of it. Then, he looked at Hugo's current condition. His face was bloody and severely swollen. In fact, both of his eyes were nearly swollen shut; his nose was broken, and he had a mouthful of broken teeth. Hugo was in so much pain and had lost so much blood that he was having trouble staying conscious. Every now and then his head would dip, but he'd throw it back up. The poor son of a bitch was fearful of waking up to being brutally beaten by the two degenerate fucks inside of the office with him.

Buck Wild couldn't understand how Hugo's big ass would still be alive after the level of savagery that he and Country had brought upon him. He had to salute his G because he thought he would have broken by now. But he'd proven that he was one tough son of a bitch and he could take it just as good as he could give it.

"Country," Buck Wild addressed him without taking his eyes off of Hugo.

"What's up, dog?" Country asked and took a drink of his water.

"How long we been up here getting in this nigga's ass, homeboy?"

Country glanced at his watch and said, "Shiiiiit, nigga, we've been up here whooping on his big bitch-ass for, like, I don't know, say, uhhh, two to two and a half hours."

"Damn, this spic is as tough as a bag of rusty old nails," Buck Wild claimed, while looking over him and Country's handiwork. They'd done a serious number on Hugo. "This mothafucka is not gonna talk. If he was, he woulda been done told us where his punk-ass boss is."

"Say, dog, I'ma have to agree witcha on that." Country burped and sat the empty bottle of water beside him. He then took a sandwich wrapped in foil from out of the cooler, and started unwrapping it. "You may as well gon' head and put that nigga there outta his misery. I mean, his big ol' ass done suffered enough, ya feel me? May as well gon' and cap his ass and give 'em a burial of a G. Shit, that's the least we could do. Ain't too many real G's left in the game. You know what I'm saying?" He took a bite of his sandwich and started munching on it.

"Yeah, I feel where you're coming from, but I got one more ace up my sleeve before I send this big fella to that great big ol' Mexican border in the sky." Buck Wild finished his bottled water and threw it at Hugo's head. The empty bottle ricocheted off of Hugo's head and fell to the floor at his feet.

Buck Wild walked over to the side of the room and picked up a black box that was on the side of a lunchbox. He sat the black box down on the desk top and popped open its locks, lifting its lid. Inside, wedged in a rectangle placement of light-gray velvet, there was a shiny metal syringe containing a clear liquid serum. Smiling wickedly, Buck Wild removed the syringe and pulled its cap off with his teeth. He spat the cap far across the office and squirted some of its serum from out the tip of its needle.

"Dog, what the fuck is that?" Country asked, frowned up. He'd never seen any shit like that before inside of a syringe that big. A hundred things of what the contents of the syringe were went through his mind. He was killing himself trying to guess exactly what it was; so he said *fuck it,* and asked.

"A truth serum," Buck Wild told him over his shoulder before he bit down on the shaft of the syringe. He unbuckled his leather belt and pulled it free from the loops of his navy blue Dickie jumpsuit. He looped the belt around Hugo's forearm and smacked it until a green vein became pronounced. Licking his thumb, Buck Wild rubbed his saliva on top of Hugo's vein before easing the needle inside of it. He pulled back on the plunger of the syringe, and some of Hugo's blood rushed into the shaft of the syringe. After waiting a moment, Buck Wild slowly began to push the truth serum into the vein of Hugo's arm. The serum reacted fast. Hugo's heart beat slowed, and he began breathing calmly.

"Is that what it's called?" Country asked, with a swollen cheek of food.

"That's actually just a simpler way of saying it. I mean imagine saying sodium thiopental every time a country-ass nigga such as yo'self asks what this stuff is." Buck Wild glanced over his shoulder at Country who held up the middle finger at him. He grinned and focused his attention back on Hugo. He looked sleepy, as his head bobbed around, and he drooled from the corner of his mouth. His pupils moved around lazily, and he looked drowsy. "Yeaaaah, it's starting to work its magic now."

"Exactly how does that shit work anyway?" Country asked before taking another bite of his sandwich.

"It makes it difficult to perform high-functioning tasks, like, uh, walking a straight line or lying. See, you need concentration to think up a lie, and sodium thiopental, the truth serum—it takes it away from stubborn mothafuckaz like this here." He nodded toward Hugo who was still moving about like he was sleepy and struggling to stay awake.

"Damn, best not let my baby mama get a hold of that shit," Country said, continuing to eat his sandwich.

Buck Wild chuckled and shook his head. He planted a chair in front of Hugo and straddled it backwards. "Yo', my man! My man!" he called for Hugo's attention, but Hugo wasn't focusing his attention on him. He was looking off to the side and saying gibberish. Frustrated, Buck Wild leaned forward and smacked him twice, each time harder than the last. Finally, Hugo focused his attention on him in a lazy manner. "Okay, big man, tell me where I can find Joaquin."

Hugo looked like he was struggling to say something, which was most likely going to be a lie, but his lips wouldn't cooperate with him. He winded up telling the truth, which was exactly what Buck Wild wanted. "Joaquin—Joaquin is at—is at—is at home—"

"Oh, yeah? Well, where's *home*?" Buck Wild inquired. It took some time but Hugo managed to tell him where he could find Joaquin. A wicked smile spread across Buck Wild's face, having gotten the information he desired. "Good looking out, my boy." He extended his balled fist for dap.

Looking at Buck Wild's fist, Hugo mad-dogged him and harped up mucus. He threw his head forward and spat a loogie in his face. Buck Wild was pissed off, but he tried to combat his anger. He clenched his jaws and balled his fists tight. That wicked smile spread across his face again, and he wiped away the loogie with his shirt's sleeve.

"Country," Buck Wild called out to his crime partner, keeping his eyes on Hugo, still smiling wickedly, "Come tell our friend here goodbye."

"Alright," Country replied with a mouthful. He munched down the rest of his food and wiped his mouth with a napkin. Next, he pulled a pair of black latex gloves over his hands and picked up his pistol with the silencer on its barrel.

Casually, he strolled over to Hugo who was now mad-dogging him.

"Fuck you, fuck you! Fuck both of you mothafuckaz!" Hugo roared, spit flying off his lips. His face turned red, and veins bulged all over his bald head.

Country lifted his pistol and pointed it at the left side of Hugo's chest. He shot him in the heart and put two in his cabbage, sending him to a fiery place called Hell. After he laid down his murder game, Country took the time to admire his handiwork and tossed the pistol he'd used to murk Hugo at his feet. He then peeled off his latex gloves and shoved them into his pocket to discard later.

"Let's roll," Buck Wild said, turning around with the cooler.

"Man, I gotta take a shit," Country said, following Buck Wild toward the door.

"Nigga, all yo' big country ass do is eat, sleep and shit," Buck Wild told him.

"And fuck! Don't forget *fuck*," Country said, disappearing through the door behind Buck Wild.

***

God sat inside of his living room, sipping Hennessy through a straw since he couldn't drink it from a bottle due to his jaw being wired shut. A few hours ago Asad's corpse had been desecrated at his own funeral. The damage was so severe it was beyond repair, so he had to get him cremated. He'd made arrangements to pick his urn up tomorrow afternoon. On top of that, Asad's fiancée, Ammura, had been murdered by one of the goons Joaquin sent to smash him and his angels. Now, their daughter, Aziza, would grow up without both of her parents. Although he wasn't directly responsible, God couldn't help feeling that it was his fault. He wished he could turn back the hands of time, but unfortunately he couldn't. He'd have to learn how to deal with the decision he'd made.

God was so wrapped up in his thoughts that he hadn't noticed Billie sitting on his lap, until she snapped her fingers and waved her hand before his eyes.

"Where were you at just now, babe?" Billie asked with one arm hung around his neck. She took a couple drags from the blunt pinched between her index finger and thumb.

"I was just, um, I was just thinking," God said, sitting his glass of Hennessy on the end table beside him. "Lemme hit that, slim."

"This?" Billie asked with a smile, patting her crotch. "Or, this?" she held up the blunt as wisps of smoke came from it.

God smiled and shook his head, thinking of how silly Billie was. "You got jokes, baby."

"See there—That's what I've been dying to see, that smile, king," Billie said, looking into his eyes as she held his chin. Her eyes were serious. "I miss that. I miss that so much." She kissed him twice on the lips and caressed the side of his face. He then took the blunt from her and took a few drags from the end of it, blowing out a cloud of smoke up at the ceiling.

"I'm sorry, queen. Considering everything that's been going on, a nigga find it kinda hard to smile and shit. You feel me?" God asked, taking another drag from the blunt.

"I know, sweetheart—I know," Billie said, as she played with his curly hair. "I just want you to remember that no matter how hard times get—that I always got cho back and yo' front. I ride or die for mine."

"Thank you, baby, I appreciate chu more than you

know." He gave her a peck and continued to smoke.

"So, who's gonna keep Aziza from now on?" Billie inquired.

"Her grandmother, Asad's mother," God told him.

"I feel so sorry for that lil' girl, you know? I mean, both of her parents are dead." Billie shook her head, thinking how it was a shame that Asad and Ammura had been murdered. "I know what that feels like. It's a horrible, awful feeling. You feel like, you feel like—you're all alone in the world. And no matter how hard your family tries to convince you of how much they love you and have your back—you can't help wondering what having the love of your parents would be like." Billie hadn't noticed she'd become teary eyed, until she felt God studying her face and wiping the wetness from the corner of her eye.

"Believe me, slim—I know exactly how that feels—all too well," God assured her before kissing her cheek. She took the blunt from him and started smoking it. "The girls still up?"

Billie shook her head and said, "No. They went to bed half an hour ago."

Right then, God's cell phone vibrated and rang. His forehead furrowed as he looked at its screen. It was Buck Wild. He answered it. "'Sup, nigga? Good. See if you can get some intel. Peace." He disconnected the call and sat his cell phone on the end table. Buck Wild had just informed him that he and Country had snatched up Hugo in so many words. He'd told him to find out where Joaquin was holed up.

"Who was that?" Billie asked curiously.

"Buck Wild and his nut-ass cousin," God told her.

"Oh, well, what did he want?"

God gave her a knowing look which she picked right up

on. She knew then that Buck Wild and Country had either caught up with Joaquin, or they had someone that could tell them where he was. Billie suddenly felt bad, thinking of how she went along with him having her child's father killed.

"You know, I was hoping that this thing between you and Joaquin would blow over, but I guess I was foolish to think that," Billie said.

"With the amount of blood that's been shed between us—Nahhh," God shook his head, like, *no way.* "This thing of ours won't be dead until I've knocked ol' boy's head off."

Billie nodded understandingly. Although that's not what she wanted to hear from him, she understood his position in the matter. Had she been the one in God's shoes, she'd want Joaquin dead too; so she couldn't blame him.

"Listen," God turned her face toward him so they'd be eye to eye. "I know you're conflicted, with him being who he is to you. But I promise you, once this is over, I'm gonna dedicate the rest of my life to making you and the girls the happiest you've ever been. You have my word. Okay?" Holding her gaze, he waited for her response. She nodded, and he kissed her. "Lemme up." He gently smacked her on her thigh, and she got up from his lap.

"Where you headed, babe?" Billie inquired, as she sat down in the spot that God was, crossing her legs.

God stopped his stride and looked over his shoulder at her. "With Asad outta the picture and Buck and Country occupied, I've gotta be the one to make sure the product gets to the cook houses."

"Couldn't you have one of yo' other workers do it? I mean, shit, you're a boss—you shouldn't be getting your hands dirty with that. Let them other fools take the risk, that's what chu paying them for."

"You're right. It's just that I don't trust anyone outside

of my three amigos with my shit. I let one of the others handle this—and they may run off with the merchandise. You feel me?"

"Yeah, I feel you," Billie said. "But them niggaz know better than to do that. Them boys pulla stunt like that and they won't just have you to worry about, but your missis. And you know how I give it up. Make a bitch come up outta retirement to let 'em know it's real." Her tone was serious. If there were two things she didn't play about, it was her family and her money.

God smiled at her. "I married myself a real one, huh?"

"The realest, boo." Billie focused her attention back on the flat screen, activating the Netflix app.

God turned into the hallway, and he could have sworn he saw someone dart into the girls' bedroom. His brows furrowed, wondering who might have been up, so he decided to check in on them. The door to their bedroom was already cracked open, so he took a peek inside. As far as he could tell, the girls were still asleep; so he chalked up what he thought he'd seen to him needing some sleep.

God closed the door shut and headed down the hallway to the bedroom he shared with Billie. He tucked his blower, slipped on his hoodie, and grabbed the big duffle bag from the back of his closet. The plan was for him to drop by his stash house to pick up the work, drop it off at the cook houses for it to be rocked up, and then he was going to head right back home.

God turned out the light inside of the master bedroom and journeyed into the living room. He gave Billie a goodbye kiss and promised to be back as soon as he finished handling his business.

***

Annabelle's eyes peeled open once she sensed God had finally left the bedroom. This was the second time she'd overheard him and her mother discussing killing her father. She hadn't mentioned to her father what she'd heard the first time, but she wished she had. The only reason she hadn't was because she thought she may haven't heard what she thought she'd heard. This was due to the fact that she was half asleep the night she'd eavesdropped on her mother and her husband's conversation.

Annabelle hoped and literally prayed that she hadn't heard right that night. But hearing her mother and God talking about executing her father again, she was sure she'd heard right this time. Although Annabelle loved God, she loved her father more naturally. She'd rather see him and her mother dead before she saw her old man laid up in a coffin. With that in mind, Annabelle turned over in bed and took the cell phone from beneath her pillow. She powered it on and looked inside of the contacts at the only number listed, *Daddy*. The night Joaquin and God had fought, he'd given it to her when he'd tucked her in and read her a bedtime story. She was to contact him if she ever needed him, and she figured now was as good a time as any.

Annabelle dipped her head under the covers to shield the light of the cellular's screen from the darkness. She listened closely as the phone rang. Joaquin finally answered.

"Hey, daddy's baby," Joaquin spoke into the phone.

"Hey, daddy," Annabelle greeted him sadly.

"Princess, what's wrong?" Joaquin questioned with concern. He could tell by the emotion in her voice something was wrong.

"D—Daddy, he wants to—wants to kill you—" Annabelle broke down crying, tears coating her cheeks.

"Hold on, baby girl. Who are you talking about, huh? Who wants to kill me?" he asked, worried. He wasn't only concerned about his welfare but that of his daughter. The way he figured it, if someone wanted to take his life, then they more than likely wanted to harm his daughter as well.

"Ky—Kyree, daddy. And mommy—mommy is gonna let 'em. I—I overheard them talking, and she's—she's okay with him doing it." Annabelle broke down crying again. She was terribly afraid of losing her father. She loved him dearly. As a matter of fact, she loved him more than she loved her mother. Little mama was a daddy's girl, through and through.

Chapter 13

When Joaquin got off the jack with Annabelle, he was hurt and devastated. It was hard for him to conceive the fact that the only woman he'd ever loved gave the okay for her new man to smoke him. He'd loved her with all of his heart and soul. They didn't necessarily have the best relationship on account of his infidelities, but he'd always believed she cared for him tremendously. Sadly, he realized he was terribly mistaken. Because if she truly loved him, there wasn't any way that she'd allow God to kill him. Not only would he be killing her first love; he would be killing her child's father.

Joaquin stood where he was holding his cell phone at his side, staring ahead at nothing. Tears slowly accumulated in his glassy eyes and spilled down his cheeks unevenly. A teardrop fell from his chin and splashed on the floor beside his foot. He shut his eyelids, and more tears coated his cheeks. Joaquin was overwhelmed with grief. The bombshell Annabelle dropped on him felt like a punch to his gut. He wished he could forget what he knew, but that was impossible. Besides, the way he looked at it, him knowing someone was out to body him put him a step ahead of them. He'd rather have this intelligence than to be ignorant of the danger awaiting him.

Due to the circumstances, Joaquin's back was against the wall. He had been forced to make a decision he wished he didn't have to make, but he really didn't have a choice in the matter. The way he looked at it, it was either him or the people that wanted to see him dead. He'd never been the kind of nigga to let another man decide his fate, and he wasn't about to start being that nigga now. Joaquin's eyebrows sloped, his nose scrunched up, his nostrils flared, and he clenched his jaws. He wiped his wet face with the fist he held his cellular in, and decided to make a phone call that would undoubtedly change his life and Annabelle's. Still, he knew he had to take action and do what had to be done.

Fuck it. It is what it is, Joaquin thought, as he searched his contacts for the number he was looking for. Once he found it, he pressed it and brought the cell phone to his ear. "Murtaugh, I needa holla at chu, my nigga. Yeah, I need you to plan a family vacation for me—"

***

Murtaugh was sitting outside of God's crib, listening to Cypress Hill's "How I Could Just Kill a Man" while smoking a joint. His eyelids were shut, and he was nodding, zoning out. You know, getting into the mind frame of a cold-blooded killa. Murtaugh had his hands in many deaths, being a crooked-ass corrections officer, but it was rare for him to get his hands dirty. He'd gotten busy at Tomas's mansion with Alvaro's goons, and here he was again—about to murder an entire family. He'd convinced himself that what he was doing was a necessary evil. Once they'd gotten rid of God, Billie and Charity, Joaquin would get sole custody of Annabelle. Then they'd have full reign over the city, and they could move their product without interference from other drug crews. Joaquin was already in the midst of making a deal with the police to look the other way while they did their thing, so in a minute they wouldn't have them to knock their hustle.

Still nodding to the music, Murtaugh mashed out what was left of his joint and slipped his hands inside a pair of black leather gloves. He took a Steyr AUG assault rifle from underneath the driver's seat, and chambered a live round into it. After sticking two fully loaded magazines for the automatic weapon in the pocket of his jacket, Murtaugh pulled a black ski mask down over his face and hopped out of the car. Shutting the door as quietly as he could behind him, he looked up and down the street for any oncoming cars. When he didn't see any coming, he jogged across the street to leave a murder scene that would surely make every news channel in the country.

***

Meanwhile, back at the warehouse—

Hugo sat with his head hanging off the back of the chair he was bound to. His eyes were wide, and his mouth was hanging open. Having been dead for hours, his complexion was powder blue, his lips were purple, and his eyes were cloudy. The gunshot wound in Hugo's forehead had oozed blood down his nose and dried. The two gunshot wounds in his chest left a big bloody stain on his shirt. Two flies swarmed around him in a circle, and one eventually landed on his face, rubbing its limbs together. There was a big fat brown rat on his shoulder, sniffing him while a big fat dark-gray rat was crawling up his pants leg. His cell phone vibrated and rang repeatedly inside his pocket. Once it stopped ringing, it would start back up again and then again. His cellular vibrated and rang six more times before the caller gave up.

***

"Qué diablos pasa con este negro Hugo, hombre? (*What the fuck is up with this nigga Hugo, man?*)" Joaquin hung up from calling Hugo's business cell phone. He'd hit up his personal cell, but it kept going straight to voicemail. Frustrated, Joaquin stuck his cellular inside of his pocket and walked toward an enormous tenement that Aztec had forced the owner to sign over at gunpoint on his behalf. Joaquin had several surveillance cameras installed in and around the building to watch everyone coming and going. He also had armed security guards with attack dogs patrolling the grounds of it. Most of the complex's tenants worked for Joaquin either as security guards, hittaz, slingers, or whatever he assigned them to do.

The tenement was really a front for something more illegal going on below the foundation of it. Deep within the bowels of the building there was a laboratory of sorts that had been funded by Tomas's drug money. It was Joaquin's brainchild, and he was one hundred percent positive that he was going to get one hell of a return on his investment.

Joaquin punched in the code on the key-pad to gain access to the tenement. The black gate buzzed and he opened the door, walking inside. He made his way to the double glass doors, nodding in acknowledgement to the armed security guards on his payroll. He made his way inside of the building, and hopped on the elevator. He pulled out a special bronze key and used it to open a small square compartment, which was below the numeric buttons of the panel. When he opened the compartment, there was a big red button with the capital letter 'U' on it. The 'U' stood for underground. He pressed that button and closed the compartment's door.

The elevator slightly shook and made an eerie sound. It traveled down toward his destination. While enroute, Joaquin's cell phone vibrated and chimed with a new text message. He glanced at his cell, and saw it was from Aztec. He was asking where he was. Joaquin hit him back with his whereabouts, and put his cellular away. Right then, the elevator's door slid apart and he stepped out, cracking open a grape swisher sweet. He made his way down a long, well-lit corridor that led to a large metal door, with a digital key-pad.

Joaquin dumped the guts of his blunt inside of a trash can. He pulled out a see-through baggie loaded with green kush covered in purple crystals. He'd already broken down the weed and removed its seeds. All he had to do now was, prepare his blunt with it. Joaquin stopped at the large door that his lab was behind. He took the time to sprinkle the kush inside the blunt. Next, he opened the door by placing his hand flat down on the digital hand-impression reader. There was a clicking, and then an air compression sound, which signaled that the door was finally open. Joaquin switched hands with his blunt, and pushed his way inside.

***

God dropped off the work to all the cooks on his payroll except Ms. Jones. He had expected to be in and out of her crib so he could head back to his own to get some sleep, but she wasn't answering her front door. He hit up the cell phone he'd given her repeatedly, and was sent straight to voicemail. He tried to leave her a message, but her mail box was full. God decided to try her front door again. Once again, he didn't get an answer; so he traveled to the side of the house, and tried to peek inside though the window. He could see the light inside of the kitchen was still on, but he couldn't see anyone moving around.

He decided to try his luck with the back door. He tossed his duffle bag over and climbed the gate, jumping down into the back yard. Snatching up his duffle bag, he made his way upon the back porch and tried the doorknob. His forehead creased, seeing that the door was already open.

Something is up! Momma Jones never leaves her shit unlocked.

God slipped the strap of the duffle bag over his neck and pulled his gun from his waistline. He cocked it and slipped inside the back door, moving through the kitchen with the skill of a police officer. The kitchen looked normal, but he could see from where he was standing that the living room looked like a cyclone had been through it. God could tell a struggle had taken place from the flipped over sofa, the toppled lamp, the broken vase, the knocked over coffee table, the portrait hanging crooked on the wall, and the cobweb in the flat screen TV.

Tough old bird—she didn't go quietly. From the look of things, she put up one hell of a fight, God thought as he looked over the messy living room. *Lemme check out the rest of this house before I get outta here.*

God took a step forward and felt something crack underneath his sneaker. His forehead crinkled, as he wondered what he'd stepped on. He removed his sneaker from what he'd stepped on to uncover Ms. Jones' scorched and scarred crack pipe. He picked it up, and his eyelids narrowed into slits, examining it closely. It still had crack rocks in it that appeared to be melted. That meant Ms. Jones was in the middle of getting high when *whoever* ran up in her crib and kidnapped her.

Yeah, somebody definitely snatched up my OG, that's for damn sure.

God's eyebrows slanted, his nose wrinkled, and he clenched his jaws. He was so angry he squeezed the crack pipe in his fist until it snapped, crackled and popped. He threw its remains aside, brushed his hand off on the leg of his jeans, and made his way out of the house, determined to find out what happened to Ms. Jones.

I know who has her—that bitch-ass nigga Joaquin. I love Momma Jones. Since I've been running these streets, she's always been like a mother to me. I swear on everything I love, if homeboy has harmed so much as a hair on her head, I'ma kill his vindictive ass.

***

Joaquin stood out on the tier, rolling himself a fat ass blunt expertly. Taking the blue flame of his lighter, he swept it back and across the blunt, sealing it closed. He placed the blunt between his lips, and cupped his hand around it, lighting it up. Joaquin sucked on the end of the blunt and made the tip of it glow amber. He blew out a cloud of smoke and looked over his budding business. A smile spread across his face, thinking of what his hard work was doing for him.

Man, shit is really starting to come together for yo' boy. I've had to shed a lot of blood in my lifetime, but that was all to propel someone else into a position of power. Now, the blood I'll shed will be for me to be top dog, Joaquin thought, as he continued to smoke his blunt. He was about to take another drag from it, when he heard a voice at his back.

"Lemme hit that!" Aztec said from behind him. His un-announced presence startled Joaquin, and sent him into a coughing fit.

Holding his fist to his mouth, Joaquin looked over his shoulder to see Aztec approaching. The little man was smiling broadly, looking quite amused by his scaring of his street brother.

"Ol' punk-ass, I scared yo' ass, didn't I?" Aztec gave a throaty laugh, doubling over and holding his stomach.

"Whatever, lil' nigga!" Joaquin said, sticking his blunt

in his mouth. He slid into a fighter's stance, throwing playful punches and jabs at Aztec. Aztec slid into a fighting stance and started throwing playful punches at him also. They danced around the top tier, laughing and horsing around like blood brothers do.

Having grown tired of playing, Joaquin stopped and took his blunt from out of his mouth. He dumped some of its grayish black ashes from the tip of it, and embraced Aztec with a one-armed hug.

"On some real shit, lemme hit that though, bro," Aztec said seriously, and extended his hand for the blunt, which Joaquin passed to him.

"Yo', you took care of that business for me, right?" Joaquin inquired about the task he'd assigned to him.

Aztec nodded and blew out smoke. "Yeah, I took care of it."

"That's why you're my nigga, Tec. You stay on yo' shit."

"I gots to, I'm your soldado."

Joaquin nodded understandingly and said, "Where Hugo and Murtaugh?"

"I just got off the teléfono with Murtaugh, said he's in-disposed—whatever the fuck that shit means. Here." Aztec passed the blunt back to Joaquin. He watched, as the man he looked up to as a big brother looked over his facility proudly. He looked like a king looking over his kingdom.

"Why are you smiling like a pedophile at a four-year-old boy's birthday party?"

"One day I'm gonna run this world, Tec," Joaquin swore, as he dumped the ashes from his blunt and took a pull from it. "Today it will be the city, but tomorrow—tomorrow it will be the entire goddamn world. And that's on my granny's daughter." He continued to take in the fruits of his labor from where he stood out on the tier, admiring everyone and everything in it.

"You've got all of this coke, so now what?" Aztec said, shrugging. "You plan on being Scarface or something?"

"You've always thought too small, baby boy," Joaquin told him. "Fuck Scarface, my nigga, I'ma be Sosa!"

Aztec nodded understandingly and said, "Street dreams."

Joaquin hung his arm around Aztec's neck and looked down, taking pulls from his blunt and blowing smoke into the air.

"Nah, not any more, lil' bro, Tomas helped me turn that dream into a reality." Joaquin smiled, as he assured him. "This is a five-million-dollar underground crack manufacturing lab. This right here is an engineering masterpiece, my nigga. Its right underneath a one hundred unit apartment complex and it's equipped with a state-of-the-art filtration system to evacuate toxic fumes; it's also capable of cooking between one hundred to three hundred pounds of cocaine a week."

Aztec leaned over the guardrail to get a closer look at the operation below. "Damn, this is—this is the most beautiful thing I've ever seen."

Below the tier there was a super lab where machine gun toting goons walked around, keeping an eye on things. All of the crackheads Murtaugh and Hugo had kidnapped were working to produce crack cocaine. The fiends—male and female—were topless, wearing only a head covering, latex gloves and an apron. They all wore a tracking device collar around their neck. The small black box attached to it had a blue light on it, which let any observer know it was functioning and its wearer wasn't out of bounds. The tracking device also acted as a shock collar, and would explode if you tampered with it.

On the main floor, inside the room on the left, there were fiends cutting crack into five-dollar, ten-dollar and twenty-dollar-sized rocks. Inside the room on the right side of the main floor, there were fiends bagging up the rocks. Once the merchandise was finished being packaged, it was loaded into the back of vans. The product was then driven to specific locations where it would be distributed out of a crack house, or slung on the corners by D-boys. At the end of every business week, *The Collectors* would be sent out to pick up the profits from the drug sales, which would then be driven out to a well-guarded count house. Later, the dirty money would be deposited into different bank accounts overseas that the federal government couldn't fuck with.

Ms. Jones stood in the room alongside other crackheads chopping up rocks to be bagged. The old head looked the same, save for her hideously scarred back she'd gotten on account of Aztec whipping her mercilessly. She'd refused to give up her recipe for cooking the illegal substance that the streets loved, so it was up to the little gangsta to break her. To her credit, she didn't give up the ingredients until he'd threatened to rape Charity right before he slit her throat.

Ms. Jones was willing to call his bluff, until she saw the seriousness in her eyes, and the sadistic smile on his face. There wasn't any doubt in her mind that he'd go through with his threat, so she told him what he wanted to know. She was then forced to show the other crackheads how to cook the product like she did. Afterward, she rotated between the assignments all of them were given inside of the lab.

Ms. Jones' eyes shifted around the room to see if the guards were watching her as she chopped off a dime sized rock. She balled the rock inside of her fist and pretended to be cutting more. Once she saw that the guards weren't paying attention to her, she swiftly tossed the rock inside of her mouth and swallowed it. She had plans of passing the rock on through a bowel movement later and smoking it. Ms. Jones went to chop another rock with the Gemstar razor, and the stock of a machine gun slammed into the side of her head. She winced as the side of her head ricocheted off the ground. Slowly, she turned over on her back and saw double of one guard standing over her, with his machine gun. By the menacing look on his face, she could tell he was pissed.

"You think I didn't see that, whore? Spit it out! Go on, spit it out! Or, so help me I'll carve it outta your belly." The guard switched gloved hands with his machine gun and pulled out a bowie knife. His hostile eyes bored into Ms. Jones', as he slowly approached her. A terrified look was on her face, as she backed up into the corner of the room, on the palms of her hands and the balls of her feet.

The other crackheads continued to chop up the drugs, while nosily paying attention to what the guard was about to do to Ms. Jones. Though some of them wanted to help her, neither of them was foolish enough to make a move. They were too fearful of being dealt the same fate as her.

"You've got 'til the count of five," the guard warned her, and started counting down. "One—"

Ms. Jones got down on her hands and knees toward the guard. She stuck two fingers as far inside of her mouth as she could, trying to make herself throw up the crack rock she'd swallowed. She gagged and coughed, as tears streamed down her cheeks. A river of murky saliva with food particles in it spilled out of her mouth and splashed on the floor. Ms. Jones looked back and forth between the approaching guard and what she was vomiting.

"Two, three—" the guard continued to count down. He clutched the bowie knife in his hand firmly and prepared to strike Ms. Jones, if she didn't present him with the crack she'd swallowed.

A couple of the crackheads shook their head in pity for her while others crossed themselves in the sign of the crucifix.

"Four, five—Time's up!" the guard said and snatched Ms. Jones up by the front of her apron, pinning her to the wall. He wrapped his hand tightly around her neck, causing her to hold onto his wrist. She made an ugly face, as she tried to loosen his hand from around her throat, which was stopping her from getting oxygen.

The guard cocked the hand back that clutched the bowie knife. He went to stab Ms. Jones so he could open up her stomach and get the rock she'd swallowed. She squeezed her eyelids shut and whispered a prayer to her creator to save her life.

***

Buck Wild pulled up outside the location that Hugo had unwillingly given him, and turned his whip off. He and Country slipped on their gloves and put on neoprene masks that covered the lower half of their face. They pulled the drawstrings of their hoods and enclosed them around their heads before tying them up. Afterward, Buck Wild pulled his Tec-9 from underneath his seat and made sure it was cocked, locked and ready.

Hearing his cell phone ring, Country held up his finger for Buck Wild to give him a minute. When he saw it was his baby mama calling him, he rolled his eyes and blew his breath, annoyed.

"Man, I don't feel like hearing this bitch mouth right now, bruh. Fuck!" Country complained, as he held his cell phone.

"Who's that?" Buck Wild asked curiously.

"My punk-ass B.M., dog," Country answered him, looking down at the cellular's screen. It suddenly stopped ringing.

"Man, just holla at her once we finish handling this business. Shit not gon' take that long. We're just gon' run up in here, crush this nigga and smash out. Look, it stopped ringing anyway. Come on."

Country's cell started right back up ringing again.

"See there, dog, here Nadine ass go again—Lemme answer this shit," Country told him. "She just had my shawty, maybe something is up with 'em."

"Man, make it quick so we can squash this fool," Buck Wild said, annoyed. Country's baby mama had always been a pain in the ass, but she seemed to have gotten worse since she had his baby. With all the tricks Nadine had his cousin doing, and all the burning hoops she had him jumping through, he made up his mind to never have children of his own. As a matter of fact, he was going to set up an appointment with his PCP as soon as possible—to see about getting a vasectomy. Fuck that shit!

Buck Wild listened to his cousin go back and forth with his baby mama for the next five minutes, before he started rushing him off the phone. They exchanged '*I love yous*', and Country disconnected the call, smiling.

"I can't believe this shit. A goddamn lovesick killa. I've done seen it all." Buck Wild shook his head and ran his hand down his face.

"Fuck you mean, bruh? That's my shawty, the mother of my child."

"Nigga, y'all got one toxic ass relationship," Buck Wild told him, straight up. "All y'all do is argue, fight, and fuck!

Make up—just to do the shit all over again."

"Relationships aren't perfect, dog—You'd know that if you didn't spend yo' time running up in hoes every chance you got instead of tryna find you something real," Country said, as he slipped his ski mask over his head and adjusted the eye holes of it.

Buck Wild pulled his ski mask over his head and turned to address Country. "Man, shut cho big, dumb country ass up and get the fuck outta this car so we can kill this nigga."

Buck Wild and Country hopped out of the car, slamming their doors shut behind them. Buck Wild popped the trunk, and Country pulled out a black pistol-grip shotgun. He racked the shotgun and slammed the trunk shut.

"Nigga murdered and butchered the young homie Asad, and then had fools smoke his baby mama—Oh, yeah, nigga fa sho' getting dealt with," Buck Wild said, as he and Country jogged toward their destination.

"Fucking right, we're doing this shit for our young jit Asad," Country told Buck Wild, while extending his gloved fist toward him.

"For Asad," Buck Wild agreed and touched fists with Country.

Joaquin was a dead man!

To Be Concluded...
The Realest Killaz 3
Coming Soon

Submission Guideline

Submit the first three chapters of your completed manuscript to <u>ldpsubmissions@gmail.com</u>, subject line: Your book's title. The manuscript must be in a .doc file and sent as an attachment. Document should be in Times New Roman, double spaced and in size 12 font. Also, provide your synopsis and full contact information. If sending multiple submissions, they must each be in a separate email.

Have a story but no way to send it electronically? You can still submit to LDP/Ca$h Presents. Send in the first three chapters, written or typed, of your completed manuscript to:

**LDP: Submissions Dept
Po Box 944
Stockbridge, Ga 30281**

DO NOT send original manuscript. Must be a duplicate.

Provide your synopsis and a cover letter containing your full contact information.

Thanks for considering LDP and Ca$h Presents.

Coming Soon from Lock Down Publications/Ca$h Presents

BOW DOWN TO MY GANGSTA

By **Ca$h**

TORN BETWEEN TWO

By **Coffee**

THE STREETS STAINED MY SOUL **II**

By **Marcellus Allen**

BLOOD OF A BOSS **VI**

SHADOWS OF THE GAME II

By **Askari**

LOYAL TO THE GAME **IV**

By **T.J. & Jelissa**

A DOPEBOY'S PRAYER **II**

By **Eddie "Wolf" Lee**

IF LOVING YOU IS WRONG... **III**

By **Jelissa**

TRUE SAVAGE **VII**

MIDNIGHT CARTEL III

DOPE BOY MAGIC IV

CITY OF KINGZ II

By **Chris Green**

BLAST FOR ME **III**

A SAVAGE DOPEBOY III

CUTTHROAT MAFIA III

By **Ghost**

A HUSTLER'S DECEIT III

KILL ZONE **II**
BAE BELONGS TO ME III
A DOPE BOY'S QUEEN III
By **Aryanna**
COKE KINGS V
KING OF THE TRAP II
By **T.J. Edwards**
GORILLAZ IN THE BAY V
De'Kari
THE STREETS ARE CALLING II
Duquie Wilson
KINGPIN KILLAZ IV
STREET KINGS III
PAID IN BLOOD III
CARTEL KILLAZ IV
DOPE GODS III
Hood Rich
SINS OF A HUSTLA II
ASAD
KINGZ OF THE GAME V
Playa Ray
SLAUGHTER GANG IV
RUTHLESS HEART IV
By Willie Slaughter
THE HEART OF A SAVAGE III
By Jibril Williams
FUK SHYT II

By Blakk Diamond

THE REALEST KILLAZ III

By Tranay Adams

TRAP GOD III

By Troublesome

YAYO IV

A SHOOTER'S AMBITION III

By S. Allen

GHOST MOB

Stilloan Robinson

KINGPIN DREAMS III

By Paper Boi Rari

CREAM

By Yolanda Moore

SON OF A DOPE FIEND III

By Renta

FOREVER GANGSTA II

GLOCKS ON SATIN SHEETS III

By Adrian Dulan

LOYALTY AIN'T PROMISED II

By Keith Williams

THE PRICE YOU PAY FOR LOVE II

By Destiny Skai

CONFESSIONS OF A GANGSTA II

By Nicholas Lock

I'M NOTHING WITHOUT HIS LOVE II

By Monet Dragun

LIFE OF A SAVAGE IV

A GANGSTA'S QUR'AN II

MURDA SEASON II

GANGLAND CARTEL II

By **Romell Tukes**

QUIET MONEY III

THUG LIFE II

By **Trai'Quan**

THE STREETS MADE ME III

By **Larry D. Wright**

THE ULTIMATE SACRIFICE VI

IF YOU CROSS ME ONCE II

ANGEL III

By **Anthony Fields**

THE LIFE OF A HOOD STAR

By Ca$h & Rashia Wilson

FRIEND OR FOE II

By **Mimi**

SAVAGE STORMS II

By **Meesha**

BLOOD ON THE MONEY II

By J-Blunt

Available Now

RESTRAINING ORDER **I & II**
By **CA$H & Coffee**
LOVE KNOWS NO BOUNDARIES **I II & III**
By **Coffee**
RAISED AS A GOON I, II, III & IV
BRED BY THE SLUMS I, II, III
BLAST FOR ME I & II
ROTTEN TO THE CORE I II III
A BRONX TALE I, II, III
DUFFEL BAG CARTEL I II III IV
HEARTLESS GOON I II III IV
A SAVAGE DOPEBOY I II
HEARTLESS GOON I II III
DRUG LORDS I II III
CUTTHROAT MAFIA I II
By **Ghost**
LAY IT DOWN **I & II**
LAST OF A DYING BREED
BLOOD STAINS OF A SHOTTA I & II III
By **Jamaica**
LOYAL TO THE GAME I II III
LIFE OF SIN I, II III
By **TJ & Jelissa**
BLOODY COMMAS I & II
SKI MASK CARTEL I II & III

KING OF NEW YORK I II,III IV V

RISE TO POWER I II III

COKE KINGS I II III IV

BORN HEARTLESS I II III IV

KING OF THE TRAP

By **T.J. Edwards**

IF LOVING HIM IS WRONG...I & II

LOVE ME EVEN WHEN IT HURTS I II III

By **Jelissa**

WHEN THE STREETS CLAP BACK I & II III

THE HEART OF A SAVAGE I II

By **Jibril Williams**

A DISTINGUISHED THUG STOLE MY HEART I II & III

LOVE SHOULDN'T HURT I II III IV

RENEGADE BOYS I II III IV

PAID IN KARMA I II III

SAVAGE STORMS

By **Meesha**

A GANGSTER'S CODE I &, II III

A GANGSTER'S SYN I II III

THE SAVAGE LIFE I II III

CHAINED TO THE STREETS I II III

BLOOD ON THE MONEY

By J-Blunt

PUSH IT TO THE LIMIT

By **Bre' Hayes**

BLOOD OF A BOSS **I, II, III, IV, V**

SHADOWS OF THE GAME

By **Askari**

THE STREETS BLEED MURDER **I, II & III**

THE HEART OF A GANGSTA I II& III

By **Jerry Jackson**

CUM FOR ME I II III IV V

An **LDP Erotica Collaboration**

BRIDE OF A HUSTLA **I II & II**

THE FETTI GIRLS **I, II& III**

CORRUPTED BY A GANGSTA I, II III, IV

BLINDED BY HIS LOVE

THE PRICE YOU PAY FOR LOVE

DOPE GIRL MAGIC I II III

By **Destiny Skai**

WHEN A GOOD GIRL GOES BAD

By **Adrienne**

THE COST OF LOYALTY I II III

By Kweli

A GANGSTER'S REVENGE **I II III & IV**

THE BOSS MAN'S DAUGHTERS I II III IV V

A SAVAGE LOVE **I & II**

BAE BELONGS TO ME I II

A HUSTLER'S DECEIT I, II, III

WHAT BAD BITCHES DO I, II, III

SOUL OF A MONSTER I II III

KILL ZONE

A DOPE BOY'S QUEEN I II

By **Aryanna**
A KINGPIN'S AMBITON
A KINGPIN'S AMBITION **II**
I MURDER FOR THE DOUGH
By **Ambitious**
TRUE SAVAGE I II III IV V VI
DOPE BOY MAGIC I, II, III
MIDNIGHT CARTEL I II
CITY OF KINGZ
By **Chris Green**
A DOPEBOY'S PRAYER
By **Eddie "Wolf" Lee**
THE KING CARTEL **I, II & III**
By **Frank Gresham**
THESE NIGGAS AIN'T LOYAL **I, II & III**
By **Nikki Tee**
GANGSTA SHYT **I II &III**
By **CATO**
THE ULTIMATE BETRAYAL
By **Phoenix**
BOSS'N UP **I , II & III**
By **Royal Nicole**
I LOVE YOU TO DEATH
By Destiny J
I RIDE FOR MY HITTA
I STILL RIDE FOR MY HITTA
By **Misty Holt**

LOVE & CHASIN' PAPER

By **Qay Crockett**

TO DIE IN VAIN

SINS OF A HUSTLA

By **ASAD**

BROOKLYN HUSTLAZ

By **Boogsy Morina**

BROOKLYN ON LOCK I & II

By **Sonovia**

GANGSTA CITY

By **Teddy Duke**

A DRUG KING AND HIS DIAMOND I & II III

A DOPEMAN'S RICHES

HER MAN, MINE'S TOO I, II

CASH MONEY HO'S

By Nicole Goosby

TRAPHOUSE KING **I II & III**

KINGPIN KILLAZ I II III

STREET KINGS I II

PAID IN BLOOD **I II**

CARTEL KILLAZ I II III

DOPE GODS I II

By **Hood Rich**

LIPSTICK KILLAH **I, II, III**

CRIME OF PASSION I II & III

FRIEND OR FOE

By **Mimi**

STEADY MOBBN' **I, II, III**

THE STREETS STAINED MY SOUL

By **Marcellus Allen**

WHO SHOT YA **I, II, III**

SON OF A DOPE FIEND I II

Renta

GORILLAZ IN THE BAY **I II III IV**

TEARS OF A GANGSTA I II

DE'KARI

TRIGGADALE I II III

Elijah R. Freeman

GOD BLESS THE TRAPPERS I, II, III

THESE SCANDALOUS STREETS I, II, III

FEAR MY GANGSTA I, II, III IV, V

THESE STREETS DON'T LOVE NOBODY I, II

BURY ME A G I, II, III, IV, V

A GANGSTA'S EMPIRE I, II, III, IV

THE DOPEMAN'S BODYGAURD I II

THE REALEST KILLAZ I II

Tranay Adams

THE STREETS ARE CALLING

Duquie Wilson

MARRIED TO A BOSS... I II III

By Destiny Skai & Chris Green

KINGZ OF THE GAME I II III IV

Playa Ray

SLAUGHTER GANG I II III

RUTHLESS HEART I II III

By Willie Slaughter

FUK SHYT

By Blakk Diamond

DON'T F#CK WITH MY HEART I II

By Linnea

ADDICTED TO THE DRAMA I II III

By Jamila

YAYO I II III

A SHOOTER'S AMBITION I II

By S. Allen

TRAP GOD I II

By Troublesome

FOREVER GANGSTA

GLOCKS ON SATIN SHEETS I II

By Adrian Dulan

TOE TAGZ I II III

By Ah'Million

KINGPIN DREAMS I II

By Paper Boi Rari

CONFESSIONS OF A GANGSTA

By Nicholas Lock

I'M NOTHING WITHOUT HIS LOVE

By Monet Dragun

CAUGHT UP IN THE LIFE I II III

By Robert Baptiste

NEW TO THE GAME I II III

By **Malik D. Rice**

LIFE OF A SAVAGE I II III

A GANGSTA'S QUR'AN

MURDA SEASON

GANGLAND CARTEL

By **Romell Tukes**

LOYALTY AIN'T PROMISED

By Keith Williams

QUIET MONEY I II

THUG LIFE

By **Trai'Quan**

THE STREETS MADE ME I II

By **Larry D. Wright**

THE ULTIMATE SACRIFICE I, II, III, IV, V

KHADIFI

IF YOU CROSS ME ONCE

ANGEL I II

By **Anthony Fields**

THE LIFE OF A HOOD STAR

By Ca$h & Rashia Wilson

Tranay Adams

BOOKS BY LDP'S CEO, CA$H

<u>TRUST IN NO MAN</u>

<u>TRUST IN NO MAN 2</u>

<u>TRUST IN NO MAN 3</u>

<u>BONDED BY BLOOD</u>

<u>SHORTY GOT A THUG</u>

<u>THUGS CRY</u>

<u>THUGS CRY 2</u>

<u>THUGS CRY 3</u>

<u>TRUST NO BITCH</u>

<u>TRUST NO BITCH 2</u>

<u>TRUST NO BITCH 3</u>

<u>TIL MY CASKET DROPS</u>

<u>RESTRAINING ORDER</u>

<u>RESTRAINING ORDER 2</u>

<u>IN LOVE WITH A CONVICT</u>

<u>LIFE OF A HOOD STAR</u>

<u>Coming Soon</u>

BONDED BY BLOOD 2

BOW DOWN TO MY GANGSTA

The Realest Killaz 2

CPSIA information can be obtained
at www.ICGtesting.com
Printed in the USA
LVHW010417260821
696090LV00020B/1755

9 781952 936487